The Bridal Party

When proposal planner Riley is asked to plan a pretend engagement for an Italian billionaire, she doesn't expect to step in as his fake fiancée, too! But accepting Antonio's "proposal" sets in motion events that will not only change Riley's life, but also those of her mother and her best friend...

In Susan Meier's latest trilogy, get swept away to Italy with the bride-to-be as she accidentally falls for her pretend groom. Oops! Meanwhile, the mother of the bride takes on the father of the groom, and gets so much more than she bargained for. And the bridesmaid goes head-to-head (and lip-to-lip!) with the best man!

It's all happening in The Bridal Party!

Read the bride's story
It Started with a Proposal

And the mother of the bride's story
Mother of the Bride's Second Chance

Both available now!

And look out for the bridesmaid's story
A Kiss with the Best Man

Coming soon!

T0205053

Dear Reader,

The Bridal Party stories are proving to be some of the most interesting ones I've ever told. I was really excited when we decided the second book should be about the mother of the bride and the father of the groom falling in love. Mostly because they are older, but also because they have more experience in life. They are established financially. They know who they are as people. But that also means they have more to lose.

As parents of the bride and groom, Juliette and Lorenzo are looking at decades of holidays together, sharing grandkids, celebrating birthdays. If they take a risk and investigate their powerful attraction, they could be spending many uncomfortable years being reminded of how they didn't fit, how their romance didn't work, how they made a mistake.

But, even if it works, are they willing to take a second chance on love, to put their hearts out there knowing how badly it hurts when a heart is broken?

So much risk. But isn't that what makes romance fun? The hope that the person you least expect could be the love of your life.

Happy reading,

Susan Meier

MOTHER OF THE BRIDE'S SECOND CHANCE

SUSAN MEIER

ROMANCE

Harlequin® ROMANCE

ISBN-13: 978-1-335-21605-2

Mother of the Bride's Second Chance

Recycling programs for this product may not exist in your area.

Harlequin Enterprises ULC
22 Adelaide St. West, 41st Floor
Toronto, Ontario M5H 4E3, Canada
www.Harlequin.com

Printed in U.S.A.

A onetime legal secretary and director of a charitable foundation, **Susan Meier** found her bliss when she became a full-time novelist for Harlequin. She's visited ski lodges and candy factories for "research" and works in her pajamas. But the real joy of her job is creating stories about women for women. With over eighty published novels, she's tackled issues like infertility, losing a child and becoming widowed and worked through them with her characters.

Books by Susan Meier

Harlequin Romance

A Billion-Dollar Family

Tuscan Summer with the Billionaire
The Billionaire's Island Reunion
The Single Dad's Italian Invitation

Scandal at the Palace

His Majesty's Forbidden Fling
Off-Limits to the Rebel Prince
Claiming His Convenient Princess

The Bridal Party

It Started with a Proposal

Reunited Under the Mistletoe
One-Night Baby to Christmas Proposal
Fling with the Reclusive Billionaire

Visit the Author Profile page
at Harlequin.com for more titles.

CHAPTER ONE

JULIETTE MORGAN STOOD in a grassy spot a few feet away from Dene Summerhouse in New York City's Central Park. She'd been summoned here by Antonio Salvaggio and her heart thrummed with anxiety.

Her daughter, Riley, had been dating Antonio for a few months, but they'd broken up. Juliette hadn't heard that they'd gotten back together. But Riley was a marriage proposal planner, and she scheduled a lot of the events she put together in this very gazebo. Wouldn't it just be like an Italian playboy to rashly propose instead of simply calling her daughter and apologizing?

She glanced at Antonio's grandmother, GiGi, and his dad, Lorenzo. They both looked like cats who'd swallowed the canary. Though Lorenzo was an extremely handsome man with his dark hair and compelling dark eyes—explaining where Antonio got his good looks—Juliette was not amused by the antics of this privileged family. When she'd been hustled here by Riley's videographer, she'd barely been introduced to the Salvaggios, let alone been given time to ask them what was going on.

Because she'd been shushed. *Silenced.*

It had been so long since someone shushed her that she didn't know whether to be amused or infuriated.

Infuriated was winning.

She glanced around. The beginning of the second week of November, the park's trees had lost most of their colored leaves. But the sun was warm. The day bright. It was a perfect fall day—

Oh, God. It *was* the perfect day for a proposal! She just knew that impulsive billionaire was going to ask her daughter to marry him.

Off in the distance, Juliette heard Riley's assistant Marietta's voice. "This way."

Riley said, "Really? I thought Dene Summerhouse was that way."

The Salvaggios laughed.

Juliette's suspicions heightened.

Marietta said, "You can get to it a lot of ways."

They emerged from a bank of trees. As they walked up the path to Dene Summerhouse, Antonio appeared behind the gazebo, still not visible to Riley but Juliette could see him. He wore a suit and tie and looked his absolute handsomest.

Marietta and Riley reached the gazebo and Marietta gave Riley a nudge. "We can't see much from back here. Why don't you go check out the inside, see if you can tell what the contractors will be changing or repairing."

Juliette frowned. What was Marietta talking about? There was no scheduled maintenance on Dene Summerhouse.

Riley did what she was told, ambling up the steps into the pavilion like a person so confused they just went with the flow.

Juliette's heart squeezed. Not only was Antonio going to propose, but Riley didn't know. Marietta had lured her here with a ruse!

Before Juliette could figure out a way to rescue her daughter, three violinists appeared out of nowhere, playing something soft and romantic.

Riley turned, clearly baffled, but Juliette wasn't. Her breath stuttered as Antonio climbed the steps. They'd broken up. They hadn't made up as far as Juliette knew. But the real bottom line was they didn't know each other well enough to get married.

This was all wrong.

The only hope she had was that her extremely logical daughter would say no.

Antonio got down on one knee, pulled a ring box from his pocket and said, "I love you. Will you marry me?"

Juliette held her breath.

Riley leaned down to kneeling Antonio and whispered something.

Antonio rose, slid his arms around her and pulled her close enough that he could whisper in her ear.

Riley eased back, studying his face as he kept whispering.

Clearly, Riley wasn't sure—might have even said no—and he was talking her into it.

He bumped his forehead against hers.

Riley pressed her lips together.

Juliette pressed her lips together. This was it. Her smart, logical daughter was going to say no.

Antonio opened the ring box and slid the ring on her finger.

No longer whispering, Riley said, "It's a different ring."

Antonio said, "The other one was for a fake proposal. This one is very real."

Riley smiled. "And it fits."

Then he kissed her. Riley kissed him back passionately, apparently with no thought to taking off the ring.

Juliette's face fell in disbelief. Where the hell was her smart, logical daughter?

Antonio broke the kiss, and the sound of the alleluia chorus filled the area. Thirty singing judges danced their way onto Dene Summerhouse and made a circle around them. GiGi and

Lorenzo began to applaud. Marietta and Jake, the videographer for Riley's company, stood off to the side, applauding too.

Juliette stared at them. What the hell had just happened?

She calmed herself. She didn't dislike Antonio. He was a nice guy. And he made her daughter happy. What she objected to was their getting married without really knowing each other. Still, they weren't *getting married* today. They had gotten engaged. No big deal. They could be engaged forever.

Or at least a year. Most people needed a year to plan a wedding. People in Manhattan needed two, sometimes three to reserve a good venue. In that time, her smart, logical daughter would see Antonio's flaws, his quirks, and she'd be wise enough to break it off with him, if the flaws and quirks were god-awful.

They might not be. Rich, handsome, suave Antonio Salvaggio could be a great choice for a husband for her daughter—after they'd been engaged awhile and knew each other better.

There was no reason to panic.

"Aren't you going to congratulate your daughter?"

Juliette pasted a smile on her face and turned to Antonio's father, the equally suave and handsome Lorenzo Salvaggio. "Yes. Sure. In a minute."

He frowned. His nearly black eyes grew serious and sincere. "Something troubles you?"

"No." Something troubling her was the last thing she'd admit. These people were rich, pampered, accustomed to getting their own way. If they supported this engagement, she'd have to be careful what she said to them. "I think I will go congratulate the happy couple."

Lorenzo said, *"Sì."* He put his hand on the small of her back and directed her to Dene Summerhouse.

She stiffened, but not from offense. Owning a home nursing agency, she worked with a lot of older doctors, who believed taking a woman's elbow or putting a hand on the small of their back was gallant. Those kinds of gestures never bothered her.

It was the zing that traveled up her spine when his fingers touched her that almost made her shiver.

Ridiculous really.

He kept his hand on her back the entire walk. When they reached Riley and Antonio, Lorenzo's mother, GiGi, was hugging them.

"I am so happy for you." The older woman glowed with happiness.

Not for the first time, Juliette noticed the scarf on her head. She knew GiGi had breast cancer. The last she'd heard from Riley, GiGi had been refusing treatment. If she'd begun the treatments in the time Antonio and Riley had been apart, that was good.

Riley stepped away from GiGi to hug Juliette, who squeezed her tightly. Even her successful business wasn't her greatest accomplishment. Riley was. Juliette loved her beyond what she had ever believed possible.

Though she thought it too soon for her daughter to be getting engaged, she wouldn't ruin this moment. She pulled back and said, "Congratulations!"

"Thanks, Mom."

Antonio came over and hugged Juliette.

"And congratulations to you too," Juliette said. "You'd better take good care of my daughter."

Riley groaned. "Mom, that sounds so outdated."

"Oh, I don't think so. I don't expect him to wait on you hand and foot or even to buy you chocolates and write poetry. But I know you want kids. I hope he's aware of that."

Antonio laughed. "That's what we both want. Two or three children we can raise in the villa."

Juliette's heart stuttered.

Her daughter would be moving to Italy? To live on a villa...when Riley's company was in Manhattan?

She faced her daughter. There were so many

questions and cautions Juliette wanted to issue. But this was a little too public. She would wait until they were alone when the conversation could be honest.

Antonio put his arm across Riley's shoulders. "That's why we're getting married in January."

Juliette's eyes bugged. Good God! Was it not shocking enough that her daughter was actually engaged and eventually moving to Italy… but so soon?

"January?"

"We don't want our wedding to be too close to the holidays. We want the day to be ours."

"First we make the commitment," Antonio said, smiling at Riley. "Then kids."

Juliette worked to find her voice. "Just like that?"

Antonio and Riley laughed joyfully, as if they were the two happiest people in the world. "Just like that."

GiGi left the small group to sit on a bench, and it dawned on Juliette that her health was poor enough that Antonio and Riley might be rushing the wedding to please his grandmother. It was noble to be sure. But a smart person didn't make a lifetime commitment to please someone else.

Marietta and Jake stole Riley's attention to congratulate her.

Juliette's thoughts jumped into overdrive trying to put all this together as her brain was bombarded by the terrible problems her daughter and her Italian playboy apparently had not considered.

"They're not kids."

Lorenzo's voice came from behind her, and Juliette turned. "No. They aren't." She sucked in a breath. "But a heads-up would have been nice and a chance to remind my daughter that she's got a company to run—here in Manhattan—also would have been appropriate."

"I understand that she's relocating most of the administrative work to Tuscany and leaving Marietta behind to continue work in the States."

Juliette gaped at him. "You know this?"

He frowned. The corners of his eyes crinkled. Juliette's breath stuttered. Good grief the man was gorgeous.

"It came up in casual conversation."

"Really? Riley hasn't been in Italy for weeks. How did it come up in casual conversation?"

He shrugged. "Maybe I also read between the lines a little bit." He smiled. His dark eyes sparkled with humor.

She swore if a person could blind others with their good looks, he'd be the one.

She took a breath. "She hasn't actually told you?"

"I guess not in actual words. But it's the logical thing to do and your daughter is nothing but logical."

Juliette's gaze strayed to her daughter. "She usually is."

"Look, I understand your apprehensions."

She faced him again. "You do?"

"You think the marriage is too soon?"

"I think the engagement is too soon, but I could have handled that if they'd spent enough time being engaged to get to know each other a little better."

"*Sì.*"

The first bit of hope filled her. "You agree that they should be engaged longer?"

He laughed. "Of course I do."

"What are we going to do about it?"

Riley and Antonio walked over again. Antonio addressed his father, "Are you ready to go?"

Lorenzo looked at his watch. "We have about three hours before the plane takes off." He caught Riley's gaze. "That gives you a half hour or so to pack."

Riley said, "Okay." She leaned in and kissed her mother's cheek. "I love you, Mom. I'll see you later." She turned to leave but stopped suddenly. "Actually, I was hoping you could fly to Italy this weekend, and we can start planning the wedding."

GiGi was suddenly beside her. She caught Juliette's hand. "*Sì!* We would love to have you.

Stay at the villa. We'll have every waking minute to plan the perfect wedding."

Lorenzo saw Juliette's expression fill with dread, as his mother outlined all the things they had to plan and how they'd be having the ceremony at the villa.

He swore the woman was going to faint or hyperventilate. Obviously accustomed to being the one in charge—as anyone who owned a business was—not being able to voice her opinion was killing her.

He understood. He knew how it was to raise an only child. He knew she felt a certain proprietary interest. Which was foolish. Once a child became an adult, they grabbed on to the life you'd so carefully nurtured and took it for a spin like a shiny new convertible. Various careers and lovers. A little travel. A lot of wine.

Though it seemed Juliette realized she couldn't voice the only dissenting opinion, she was still having trouble processing everything.

She said, "Sure, that's great," to Riley's invitation that she come to Italy. Then Riley, Antonio and GiGi headed out of Central Park to the limo.

Juliette stared after them.

"You wouldn't happen to be able to give me a ride to the airport, would you?"

She spun to face him. Her eyes still spoke of

confusion, but he suddenly noticed how green they were. The prettiest green he'd ever seen.

"You need a ride?"

He laughed at the incredulity in her voice. "I was kidding. They might have taken my limo, but I can call a cab." He smiled at her. "I have about an hour if you'd like to go to a coffee shop to talk this out?"

That seemed to knock her out of her shock. Her eyes sharpened. Her full lips lifted into a fake smile. If he hadn't negotiated with world-class businesspeople for the past thirty-plus years, he wouldn't have realized the smile was fake. He wouldn't have seen the determination in those eyes.

"No. Thank you. I'm fine."

He snorted. "I'm sorry, but thirty seconds ago you looked like you were going to faint. I know it's difficult when you feel left out of your child's decisions—"

"Feel left out?" She gaped at him. The fire in her eyes could have set Central Park ablaze. Her shoulders were back. Her breathing became ragged. "This morning, my daughter was snarfing down a doughnut, telling me she was considering giving up on men forever. Now she's engaged and flying to Italy? Yeah. I'm definitely out of the loop."

"Then come with us."

The eyes that had been filled with fire narrowed. "Oh, you'd love that, wouldn't you?"

"This isn't war. There's no need to think I'm planning a sneak attack. We're going to be organizing a wedding." He smiled. "Join us."

She huffed out a sigh. "No. Thank you."

She turned and stormed down the path to the street, leaving him standing at Dene Summerhouse in Central Park. When she was out of range of hearing, he let himself laugh.

She was magnificent when she was angry.

Still, unless he wanted to risk her doing something she might regret when she eventually did come to Italy, he was going to have to keep an eye on her—

Which, actually, wouldn't be a hardship. She was very pleasant to look at. He liked her eyes. He loved her hair. Yellow. Shiny.

And, no, he hadn't missed that she had the figure of Venus.

CHAPTER TWO

JULIETTE CAUGHT A cab back to her office and rode the elevator to the fifth floor, knowing she needed a few minutes alone to think this through before she said anything to anybody. Lorenzo had said this wasn't war and there was no need to think he was planning a sneak attack?

Huh!

She burst out of the elevator and charged down the corridor to the private entry to her office.

That was because his side was winning! He might not be plotting against her but there was a clear strategy in the works. He'd love for her to capitulate, fly to Italy and be the sweet mother of the bride, thrilled because her daughter was marrying above her social status—

She closed her office door and leaned against it.

Dear God. She hoped that wasn't what was really bugging her.

She sat on the tall-backed chair behind her desk and spun it to face her unremarkable view of Manhattan. Her business made lots of money, but she didn't waste it on a showy office with a view. She also shared space and a receptionist with Riley's company.

She was smart. Frugal. Did everything right.

Why? Because Riley's dad's parents had kicked her out of the condo she shared with their son when Greg died unexpectedly. From old money, they'd called her a gold digger, an upstart, and refused to acknowledge Riley.

Instead of being hurt, she'd gotten angry. She'd used that anger to make something of herself. More than something. She now had lots of money. She was well-known. Respected. No supercilious billionaire would ever look down on her again.

She sucked in a breath. All that was true. It was actually a source of pride. Who wouldn't be happy that they were a success?

But was that also why she so desperately mistrusted Antonio's family? Because they were rich the way Greg's family had been?

No. The real question was: Was that why she didn't want Riley marrying into the Salvaggio family?

Juliette tossed a pencil to her desk. No. That wasn't it either. The truth wasn't about the Salvaggio family. It was about *her*. She'd fallen for Greg too quickly. Then she'd gotten pregnant, and they'd made plans to marry...but he'd never married her.

They'd lived together for eight years. At first, getting married just seemed like nothing more than confirmation of what they already knew. They were in love. Then, as the years passed, she had to admit she had wondered why it was never the right time for them to tie the knot. She had no family, and his family wouldn't have wanted to witness them get married. They could have easily gone to the courthouse and gotten married in a quick ceremony.

But they never had. Greg always had a reason. It wasn't until he'd been dead ten years that she'd realized his "reasons" were actually excuses.

He hadn't wanted to marry her.

If she was worried about Riley, it was because she was worried Antonio would hurt her daughter the way Greg had hurt her. Greg made her feel like the most important person in the world, but he wouldn't commit—

Had he grown tired of her?

Was that why he didn't want to marry her?

Her phone buzzed. Her office assistant's voice came through the speaker. "Juliette, the weekly reports were emailed to us from the accountants. I printed them for you. Do you want to see them now or should I hold on to them?"

She rose from her desk and walked out to Jane Fineman's office. "I'll take them now."

Jane studied her face, then her brow wrinkled. "Are you okay?"

"I'm fine. Riley got engaged. That's the reason I was rushed to Central Park this afternoon."

Jane clapped her hands together. "Oh, that's wonderful!"

"Is it? She hasn't known Antonio very long."

Jane batted a hand. "I didn't know my husband long before we got engaged."

"Engaged is one thing. They want to marry in January."

"*This* January? It's already November. That's only a little over two months from now."

"I know."

Jane sucked in a breath and obviously tried to be diplomatic. "Well, lots of happy marriages begin spontaneously like that."

Juliette smiled to let her assistant off the hook. "Yes. That's true. We'll hope for the best."

She maintained that attitude, pretending to be happy, the rest of Monday and all day Tuesday, but by Wednesday morning, keeping up the pretense wore thin. She called Pete Williams, her second in command, into her office and told him she was going to Italy.

"Don't forget we have meetings with two huge doctor groups on Monday. Recommendations from them could substantially increase our business."

She rose and began organizing her cluttered desk. "I'll only stay until Sunday." She found her briefcase, opened it and slid a bunch of reports inside. "With the time difference, I'll be back on Monday morning. Email all the information I need to read before our meetings."

She went home, packed a bag, called the airline, went to the airport and was in Italy eighteen tiring hours later. Adding the hours of the flight, then a train ride and factoring in the time difference, she arrived in Florence at three o'clock in the morning Italian time.

She'd lost a whole damned day.

Luckily, she caught a cab and could check in at her hotel. She'd gotten the name of the place Riley had stayed at when she visited Antonio and arrived bleary-eyed and exhausted. As she walked through the lobby, she saw that the bar with the glass wall had only a few patrons, all of whom looked about ready to call it a night.

The desk clerk, however, was fresh as a daisy. She cheerfully checked Juliette in as if accustomed to having exhausted Americans show up in the middle of the night and then Juliette headed for the bank of elevators.

She crashed on the bed in the tiny hotel room,

then slept until noon Italian time…or six o'clock in the morning Manhattan time.

Groaning, she rolled out of bed to shower and dress for the day, then debated calling Riley to let her know she was there. In the end, she decided to wait until after she ate to give herself time to think of a reasonable excuse for why she'd flown to Italy early.

She could make it look like she was so excited to start wedding planning that she'd arrived a day early. When really, she wanted some time to talk to her daughter. Alone. She wanted the chance to explain why she should at least delay the wedding until June or July or even November of the following year so she and Antonio would have a real opportunity to get to know each other.

She would have to be crafty about spiriting Riley away for a private talk when the Salvaggio family seemed to be completely on board with this wedding—

Except Lorenzo.

He'd agreed with her that it was all too soon, and maybe she could work that to her advantage.

Lorenzo had spent the morning with his friend and business associate Marco. Though Marco was Italian, he now lived in Paris. He stayed at the same hotel every time he was in town, and usually insisted on having lunch there.

"Don't you love this place?"

Lorenzo gave Marco a sideways glance. "It's kind of Americanized."

Marco spread his hands. "So?"

"I like the United States as much as anyone, but I'm not a fan of a hamburger for lunch."

Even as he said that a pretty woman walked past the big glass wall that separated the restaurant from the lobby.

He stared for a few seconds, taking in her yellow hair and the way her blue jeans hugged her butt, then said, "You're not going to believe this but that looks like Antonio's future mother-in-law."

Marco squinted. "Oh…well, I see where Riley gets her good looks." He straightened in his chair. "Maybe you introduce me?"

Lorenzo's voice soured. "No!"

"Oh, so *you're* interested."

"No. Not because she isn't pretty, but because I think we have some trouble on the horizon. In fact—" he rose from his chair "—I might just check to see if that is her. She's supposed to be coming to help plan the wedding this weekend. There's a good possibility she decided to come a little early."

He paid their bill and raced out of the restaurant. She was nowhere in sight. Enough time had passed that the woman could have already caught a cab or rideshare. But when he returned to the lobby, he saw her at the concierge desk.

"Having a problem?"

She turned. "Lorenzo! What are you doing here?"

"My friend Marco stays here when he's in town. Though I can sometimes persuade him to go to a better restaurant for dinner, this is where he insists on having lunch."

She laughed.

He blinked. She was magnificent when she was angry, but happy she was stunning. Clearly, Riley had gotten her timeless beauty from her mother. Smooth complexion, soft eyes and the kind of mouth that teased men every time it formed a word.

He cleared his throat. "Sorry. What were we saying?"

"You were telling me about your friend Marco."

"He's in the restaurant, about to go to his room to do some work, which means I have time, if you'd like to drive out to the villa with me." He winced. "I assume you're going to the villa?"

"Actually, because of the time change, I slept all morning. I haven't had breakfast yet. I walked out of the hotel, then came back in to get a recommendation from the concierge."

"I can recommend somewhere to eat, and I will be happy to accompany you."

For a second, it looked as if she'd say no. Instead, she smiled again. "Sure. But nothing big. A bagel, croissant or doughnut would be fine."

He scoffed. "Doughnut? Really?"

"Hey, I'm just looking for enough calories to get me to dinner."

He laughed and directed her to walk to a nearby bistro. When they reached the outdoor seating, he said, "Outside or in?"

"It's a bit brisk."

"It always is in November." He motioned to the door. "Inside it is."

They chose a small table, and a server came over. Juliette ordered a croissant and coffee. He ordered a bottle of water.

As she walked away, Juliette said, "I get it. You're a health fanatic."

"Nope. I'm a person of balance. Tonight, at dinner, you will see me enjoying wine. I am able to do that because I eat right and drink water nearly all day."

"Ah, a smart guy."

She said it teasingly, but there was nothing that turned her on more than a person who looked after themselves. She watched her weight, worked out, worked hard on her business and read to keep her mind sharp. If he told her he'd read any of the recent bestsellers, she'd probably swoon.

But she couldn't swoon. She needed this guy. If one of them suggested the wedding was too soon, Riley and Antonio could brush them off. But if they had a united front, the kids couldn't ignore them.

The waitress came with her food and his water. When she was gone, Lorenzo said, "You know, I wasn't sure you'd show up this weekend."

She stopped her croissant halfway to her mouth. This could be her opening, but she'd let him talk first. See what he had to say. "Really?"

"You weren't happy about this engagement and marriage."

"I wasn't. But if I remember correctly, neither were you."

He sighed. "I think it's too soon."

"Then why aren't you fighting this?"

"Because Lorenzo is a grown man, and your daughter is also an adult."

"Meaning, we just let them make mistakes?"

"What would you like to do? Devise an evil plan?"

She laughed. "It doesn't really have to be evil." She sighed. "I'd just like twenty minutes alone with my daughter. You could also spend twenty minutes alone with Antonio and express your concerns. Or maybe we could talk to them together?"

He sat back. Juliette surreptitiously studied him. Expensive suit, white shirt, fabulous dark hair. For the first time it struck her that his hair wasn't short and businesslike as Antonio's was. It was longer, to his collar, and a little ragged, a little rough around the edges—very sexy.

"Won't that make them feel like we're ganging up on them?"

"You think we should divide and conquer?"

He snorted. "I'm still in the camp that thinks we should let our adult children make their own choices." He paused. "Though, while planning the wedding, items might come up that make them realize waiting a few months might be better."

She set down her croissant. "Such as?"

He toyed with his water bottle. "The temperatures are cold in January. They want to be married in the vineyard. They're so excited right now that it probably hasn't crossed either of their minds that they'll need to wear coats to their ceremony. No strapless dress for Riley."

She smiled. This was the better plan. "And she looks so good in a sweetheart neckline."

He chuckled. "There will also be no reception outside. Which is a shame because GiGi recently redid our outdoor space. In the summer, it would be perfect for a wedding."

"Mentioning that might get GiGi on our side."

He winced. "Don't count on it. She's a tough nut to crack. Right now, she's envisioning a blissful holiday followed by a fabulous wedding in her own backyard. All that stuff grandmas love."

She laughed. "Okay, so what are you not a fan of? Holidays or foo-foo stuff?"

"Don't get me wrong. I like celebrations. But most things are better unplanned and natural." He took a swig of water, set it down then smiled at her. "Like a woman in bed."

Dear God. Sexuality was like breathing to him. Unplanned and natural.

Her chest tightened. Her heart rate had gone wild.

She was fifty. Not dead. And he wasn't much older. He was fifty-five, tops.

He was also gorgeous. And she swore that "unplanned and natural" comment had been flirting.

The server returned with their check. Lorenzo took it and pulled a few bills from his wallet, telling her to keep the change.

Finished with her croissant, Juliette tossed her napkin to the empty plate. "Want to explain that last comment?"

"It's just an expression." He finished his water.

"You don't have to worry about me making a move on you. Imagine how awkward holidays would be if you and I had a torrid affair, then split up. We have to be together for baby births, baptisms, birthdays…and all holidays." He rose. "Cute as you are, I've decided you're off-limits."

CHAPTER THREE

LORENZO MOTIONED FOR her to precede him out of the bistro but as soon as they were outside, she turned on him. "First, no one decides anything for me. Second, cute? Seriously? I'm *cute*?"

He pulled out his phone and texted his driver. "What did you want me to say? Your beauty blinds me with its splendor?"

"Now you're just being ridiculous."

He slid his phone back into his pocket. "*Cute* implies young and perhaps impish. You might not want an evil plan, but what we are about to do is devilish."

"Okay. Fine. Whatever. Think what you like. I'm not here to have a fling with you. Just as you said, it would get awkward."

The limo arrived and he motioned for the driver to stay inside and opened the door for Juliette himself.

They slid onto the bench seat, and he pulled the door closed. "So you have flings?"

"You don't?"

"I'm Italian. It's expected of me."

"Meaning, you think an American business-woman is too what? Too busy? Too uptight to have an affair?"

He caught her gaze. "I don't really know you. You could be."

She gaped at him. "Seriously?"

Right at that moment, he would have given his life savings to kiss her. Her expressions could be so thunderous he knew that kissing her would be explosive—and real. She would give her entire self to a kiss.

Since that was wrong, for all the reasons he'd mentioned, he yanked himself out of that fantasy and shifted to look straight ahead. "Doesn't matter. We are parents of the bride and groom. We have responsibilities. *You* want to delay the wedding. We shouldn't even be thinking about kissing."

An awkward pause followed. Juliette said, "*I* wasn't."

He sucked in a breath. That was a bit of a slipup. But technically there was no harm done.

As pretty as she was, as magnificently energetic and passionate as she was, his assessment was right. There could be nothing between them.

Juliette ignored him for the duration of the ride to the villa, entranced by the raw and beautiful landscape of Tuscany in late fall. She might have asked him what was being harvested in the groves of hills they passed, but he had her too confused.

He agreed about the wedding, but he wasn't going to help.

He decreed that there would be nothing between them when she hadn't suggested there should be.

He told her they shouldn't be thinking about kissing—

When no one had mentioned kissing.

Meaning, he'd been thinking about kissing her. Even as the idea stole her breath, her brain became righteously indignant. He was a bit full of himself.

Of course, he was rich, good-looking, suave—

And he'd thought about kissing her.

The limo eased down a long driveway and stopped. Within seconds, the driver opened the back door, and she got out in front of a grand three-story yellow stucco mansion. The vineyard behind it was bare but somehow still beautiful in this resting phase. The blue sky looked down on Tuscany lovingly.

"Wow."

Lorenzo put his hand at the small of her back again. This time, knowing that he'd thought about kissing her, the jolt of electricity that flashed up her spine nearly set her sweater on fire.

"This property has been in our family for generations."

Remembering she needed him, she forgot all about the electricity and the fact that he'd thought about kissing her. A compliment could get them to a better place. And, really, that was her goal. Keeping him on her side.

"It's amazing. It's also clear your family takes loving care of your home."

"Thank you. We see it as a responsibility."

There was that word again. *Responsibility.* He thought they had a responsibility to their kids. He had a responsibility to his land.

It was interesting. She might have believed he went a bit overboard, except his sense of responsibility, maybe even duty, fit him.

Greg hadn't seen himself as having a responsibility to anybody or anything. His focus had been on making money.

It certainly wasn't on her or Riley.

That might set Lorenzo apart from Greg, but she couldn't forget that this man who was almost poetic in his love of his vineyard was cut from the same cloth as the family who had kicked her and her innocent child out on the street.

Her sense of reason restored, she allowed Lorenzo to lead her to the front door. Inside the beautiful foyer, he called, "GiGi!"

Juliette looked up, expecting to see his mother appear at the top of the grand staircase. Instead, Riley said, "We're in here."

She turned in the direction of the voice, but Lorenzo caught her shoulders and looked her in the eyes. "Are you ready for this?"

His dark eyes held hers, giving her a second to take them in and enjoy their sharpness. But she didn't stare long. He'd already thought about kissing her and she didn't want him to get the wrong idea. Plus, his question was actually encouragement of a sort. He wanted her to succeed.

"I think so. I'm going to make your weather the villain in a January wedding."

He laughed. "Good way to look at it."

"I am a fairly successful businesswoman." She slid out from under his hold. "I know how to help my staff see things the way I want them to." She took a few steps toward the room then paused and looked back at Lorenzo again. "I've also been known to charm a banker or two."

Hoping he was following her, she walked through the doorway into a room that could best be described as a family room. Bookshelves, a wet bar and lots of couches and chairs filled the room.

Riley jumped up and hugged her. "Mom! Why didn't you tell us you were coming early?"

GiGi smiled. "*Sì!* We could have had a feast tonight."

Lorenzo finally entered. His jacket gone, his tie loosened, he strode over to the wet bar. He pulled out a bottle of water. "Anyone else?"

There was a general round of refusal, as Juliette eased farther into the room to the sofa where Riley sat surrounded by open books displaying bridal gowns. Unexpected tears formed.

Her baby was getting married.

She stopped the flood of emotion. She could cry all the happy tears she wanted if Riley and Antonio waited until summer to make sure they were doing the right thing.

"I see you're looking at bridal gowns."

GiGi patted the cushion beside her, indicating Juliette should sit. When she was settled, GiGi handed one of the thick books to her. The pages weren't glossy like a magazine or catalog. They were designer drawings. Riley's gown would be an original.

Because she was marrying into a family swimming in old money.

"These are beautiful."

Riley laughed. "I would have been happy to buy something off the rack since time is so limited…but GiGi insisted we needed an original. A gown in a style no one else has ever worn."

Juliette ignored the shout of caution that exploded in her brain because Riley's comment opened an interesting door for another reason to delay the wedding. "Are you sure you'll get the gown by January?"

"Sì," GiGi said. "I will see to it."

"How?"

She laughed. "Money talks."

Discomfort stiffened Juliette's spine. Riley spoke so affectionately of this family that it was clear she didn't see the pretense all around them. Still, this wasn't the time to bring that up. Not when she could use all the issues surrounding the dress to make yet another good argument.

"Technically, as mother of the bride, I should be buying the dress." She glanced around. "Actually, doesn't the bride's family pay for the whole affair?"

GiGi batted her hand. "Don't be silly. With the wedding at the vineyard, it is our honor to foot the bill."

That hadn't worked, but it had opened another door. "The wedding's outside?"

"Just the ceremony," Riley said.

"It's cold in January. That means you're restricted in the kind of gown you can get."

"No! Look!" Riley peered around the sofa until

she found the drawing she wanted. She handed it to her mother. "Don't focus on the gown. Just the white velvet cloak." She smiled dreamily. "Look at that hood. I'm going to look like Maid Marian."

Lorenzo finally spoke. "From *Robin Hood*?"

"The remake with Kevin Costner was amazing," Riley gushed.

Staring at the cloak, Juliette reluctantly said, "It *is* beautiful."

Riley handed her drawings of three dresses. "Picture these with the cloak over them," she said helpfully, sounding so happy that Juliette's heart sank.

After another hour of discussing the three gowns, Riley wasn't able to choose from among them and they came to a stalemate. GiGi told her that they'd have the designer do quick versions of all three gowns that she could try on.

Without a pause, GiGi then showed Juliette three menus. She explained that the reception would be in the ballroom, which was down a long hall that she'd be happy to show Juliette.

In the enormous room, Antonio's grandmother pointed to spaces that would be occupied by musicians for dinner music and a band for dancing.

Walking up the hall to return to the front room, Riley talked about flowers from a local florist that she'd interviewed for her Tuscan proposal events. Marietta would be coming as a bridesmaid. Maybe the maid of honor? She hadn't yet decided how big her bridal party would be.

As Juliette took her seat on the sofa again, menus, flowers, music, gowns, cloaks, the ballroom and even the weather tumbled around in her brain like towels in a dryer. And somewhere in the mess, her wish to postpone the wedding kept getting lost.

Every time she tried to think of a way to get Riley alone or simply edge in the thought that the wedding would be prettier, happier, nicer in the summer, someone showed her a wineglass or potential napkins or a swatch of material that might become bridesmaids' dresses.

She bounced from the sofa. "You know, you guys have been looking at all this, planning things since Monday." She forced a smile. "You might have even started on the jet home."

GiGi laughed. "*Sì*, we did!"

"I need some time to catch up."

Riley's face crumpled. "Oh, Mom! I'm sorry. I didn't mean to make you feel left out."

GiGi clutched her chest. "We are so sorry."

"It's fine. Your planning isn't the problem. It's me," she assured them. "I'm jet lagged." She motioned around the coffee table filled with lists and drawings. "There's a lot of stuff going on here for a person to take in all at once." She sucked in a breath. "I should probably go back to the hotel, soak in a bubble bath, maybe go to bed early…"

GiGi frowned. "You are staying at the hotel?"

"Yes. I don't want to impose."

"It's no imposition!"

Lorenzo rose from his seat across the room. He hadn't said a word in twenty minutes. She'd almost forgotten he was there.

"I think what Juliette is saying is that she will probably be video conferencing with her staff, keeping up with her work while she's here. It's better she have a room in a hotel."

"And the jet lag," Juliette reminded them, trying to mitigate appearing rude. She needed time to regroup.

"You are not staying for dinner?"

"I will tomorrow. I promise. Honestly, I'm simply tired."

Riley hugged her.

GiGi warmly said, "We will see you tomorrow," and Lorenzo got her out of the house.

"They overwhelmed you?"

"Yes."

The limo pulled up. Juliette was so flummoxed she hadn't even noticed him texting for it. He opened the door. She slid inside and he followed her.

"I'm sorry. I hope I didn't offend your mother."

"She's a tough old girl. It takes more than that to faze her."

She leaned back on the beach seat. "Not only did I not get any of my points across, but I made myself look like a fool."

"You were fine until GiGi started talking about the flatware, then I think your brain was too full to take in anything else."

"They planned the whole wedding."

"They came up with *ideas* for the whole wedding. Tomorrow when your jet lag is gone, you can give your opinions. Talk things over with Riley, as any mother would when she and her daughter are planning her wedding."

"You think?"

He glanced over. "You don't?"

"Even though I'm trying to delay this—and disagreeing with their choices could start the ball rolling in that direction—I don't want to be that pushy mother who wants everything her way. Plus, I would like to be a part of things if I can't get them to wait until June."

"Makes sense. But it might be fun to see bossy Juliette come out and go toe-to-toe with GiGi about the musicians or the flowers."

She laughed. "No. It wouldn't. And I'm not always bossy."

He gave her a sidelong glance again. "You sure?"

She snorted. "Yes."

"I like your bossy side. I'm guessing it comes from years of running a company."

"It does. Before that I was a sweet, naïve girl. I lived with Riley's father for eight years and we never had a cross word."

"Wow. My wife and I were together for less time than that, and she used to throw dishes at me."

Juliette laughed.

He pointed at his temple. "I've got a wicked scar to prove it."

"Why'd you marry her?"

He sighed wistfully. "Ahh, she was *pretty*. And really something at parties. Everyone adored her. After we got married, I realized she was always effervescent and bubbly because she was always buzzed."

"Close to drunk but not quite there?"

"Yes. Thus, her ability to still be able to toss a dish." He sucked in a breath. "Didn't figure out she had an alcohol problem until after Antonio was born."

She shook her head. "You act like your life together was no big deal. But I know how hard it probably was. I run a home nursing agency. We've dealt with our share of addictions."

"I knew the marriage was over when Antonio was only two years old. It wasn't difficult to lose her when the time came and that made me sad." He peeked at her again. "What happened to you and Mr. Perfect."

She sniffed. "He wasn't perfect. We just seemed to fit."

"But…"

"But he died."

"Oh, I'm sorry! I remember Riley telling us that. I shouldn't have mentioned it."

"Yeah, well, that's how I ended up becoming tough. His family kicked us out of our condo, refusing to acknowledge Riley and calling me a gold digger." She snickered. "Their hate motivated me to become the best and in my own way I am."

"We sure have a lot of baggage between us."

This time she full belly laughed. "Because we've lived longer than single people in their twenties or thirties." She nudged his shoulder. "But I bet we have better stories."

He leaned down and whispered, "I bet we do."

Time froze. It had probably been the jet lag that caused her to open up to him, but it didn't feel wrong. Riley had obviously told Antonio's family about her father, which was a perfectly normal thing to do. It was the closeness between her and Lorenzo that threw her. He'd all but said he'd thought about kissing her and now here he was, his lips only a few inches away.

The longing to kiss him rippled through her. She told herself it was nothing but curiosity and debated. A kiss did not have to mean they would start something—

But would a kiss be enough? He was gorgeous. His voice was smooth like a silk scarf running along her skin, raising goose bumps. Plus, she dated. She'd had months-long relationships that were sexual.

But while those guys had great careers and made big salaries, they were not in Lorenzo Salvaggio's league.

Kissing him opened too many doors to temptation that could end up hurting her. And that was reason enough to stay away from him. Particularly since being near him had the whisper of destiny.

Of course, so had her relationship with Greg—the high-society guy who couldn't quite bring himself to marry her.

Yeah. She couldn't forget that.

She eased up on the seat and scooted a few inches away from Lorenzo, refusing the temptation.

He cleared his throat and straightened up too. She took that as confirmation that he agreed with her.

But when they got to her hotel, and she was walking through the lobby, the weirdest sense haunted her. Being around Lorenzo did have a feeling of destiny about it. He was fun, good-looking and charming. Much more so than the men she'd been dating—

Was ignoring this chance really smart or was it a missed opportunity?

CHAPTER FOUR

FRIDAY MORNING, Juliette had just finished dressing when her cell phone rang. Fastening her earring, she raced to answer it, hoping it was Riley, wanting to talk. She and Riley had been close, like girlfriends, most of their lives. They'd lived together until Riley had gotten her proposal planning business on its feet. Now they shared office space and discussed every aspect of their respective companies.

Yet, suddenly, they had no time alone. No time for mother and daughter to talk things out. No time for Juliette to tactfully, respectfully, tell her daughter to wait a while before she married her handsome Italian.

She peeked at the caller ID and sighed with relief. "Riley?"

"Hey, Mom."

She sat on the bed. "What's up?"

"I think you and I need to talk."

She winced. "I'm really sorry about bugging out yesterday."

"And I'm really sorry that we seem to be planning the wedding without you. That's not at all how I wanted this to happen. In fact, I've been thinking you should leave the hotel and stay at the villa for a few weeks. We can all plan together and you can see Antonio and I are the real thing. You like him, Mom, and I love him. All you need is a little time with us to see that."

Her worst fears melted into a puddle of love for her daughter. Her smart, successful, cautious daughter. She thought of her conversations with Lorenzo the day before. Remembered that she didn't want to be the pushy mother of the bride. Remembered the look of love Riley wore every time Antonio was around.

"Oh, sweetie. That's—" She swallowed, suddenly feeling like she'd panicked prematurely. Riley *was* smart, successful, cautious. No matter how shocking that proposal had been, Riley didn't make decisions lightly. She wanted to marry Antonio. And as her mom, Juliette should be helping with the wedding, enjoying one of the happiest times of a mother's life.

"You know what? Staying at the villa is a good idea. But I can't spend two weeks in Italy until I put everything in order at work. Pete and I have a meeting on Monday with some influential doctors. I can't leave that to him alone. So how about this? How about I go back to Manhattan, go to that meeting and spend time with my staff to arrange things so that everything is set for the weeks I'm away?"

"You promised GiGi you'd have dinner with us tonight."

"I probably won't be able to get a flight out until tomorrow morning anyway. I can still have dinner with the Salvaggios tonight. I'll leave tomorrow and be back on Tuesday or Wednesday. Probably Wednesday considering the hours of travel and the time difference."

Riley's voice perked up. "That's perfect. We'll hold off on planning anything else until you return."

The hotel room phone rang. "Sweetie, the phone is ringing. I'll see you at dinner tonight."

"See you tonight."

Happier than she'd been in weeks, she disconnected her call with Riley and answered the hotel phone. "Hello?"

"It's me. Lorenzo. I came to town an hour early so I can take you to breakfast."

Even in the morning, his voice was as smooth as good whiskey. She instantly shifted from mother of the bride to woman attracted to an extremely sexy guy. Their almost kiss in the limo the afternoon before popped into her head. The sense of destiny. The fact that she could be missing out on something wonderful by ignoring all these feelings.

And the fact that she was about to spend two weeks living in his house.

This time next week, she'd be staying in his villa, enjoying being mother of the bride. She did not want to be distracted from that. Besides, he'd already said, and she'd already agreed, that anything romantic between them was off the table.

"You don't have to do that."

"I insist. Besides, I'm already here. Would it be so terrible to spend time with me?"

His voice and accent caused her hormones to shiver. She shook her head at her own foolishness. Maybe if she spent some more time with him, she'd get accustomed to him, and her unwanted feelings would go away before she found herself spending twenty-four hours a day in his company?

"Why don't we meet at the restaurant in the lobby?"

"I'm already here. I'll get us a table."

"I'll be right down."

She hung up the phone. Grabbing her purse, she left her room then rode the elevator to the lobby. She entered the restaurant and saw Lorenzo seated at a table in the back. He waved her on and rose as she approached.

"Good morning."

He pulled out her chair for her. "Good morning. I see I didn't call too early." He motioned to her soft blue sweater and jeans. "You're already dressed."

He looked cosmopolitan and sexy dressed for work in his black suit and red tie, especially with his dark hair. But she ignored the sizzle of interest that raced through her. They were nothing more than parents of the bride and groom.

"Yes. I was just finishing when you called." She positioned herself in her chair.

"Good. I wouldn't want to disturb your sleep."

Part of her would happily allow him to disturb her sleep anytime he wanted. The other part was smart enough to agree that as parents of the bride and groom, they shouldn't get involved, if only because they would be connected *forever*. They'd spend holidays together. They'd be together for the birth of every grandchild. Then they'd be together at every birthday party for those grandchildren.

If they started something and it fizzled, the rest of her life would be spent with a guy she might have been attracted to but a guy she'd broken up with. That would be amazingly awkward.

"No worries. But maybe it's good we're getting a chance to talk. Riley called this morning. She invited me to spend two weeks at your villa."

He winced. "Since you're not asking me to send a limo for your things, I'm guessing you're not okay with that."

"Actually, I am. I'm dropping my concerns about their wedding to become mother of the bride. I need to go home for a meeting on Monday, and to make sure my business can run without me for two weeks, then I'm coming here to be part of planning the wedding."

His eyes narrowed. "Really?"

She sighed. "Riley is very smart. She's also a good decision-maker. If she wants to marry your son, she's thought it through."

"Ah. You're going to let your adult daughter make her own choices."

Her goose bumps turned to porcupine quills. "You don't have to make me sound like an overprotective mama bear."

He pressed his hand to his chest the way GiGi had the day before. "I didn't mean to! It was a joke."

Her brain froze. He hadn't said or done anything to warrant her snapping at him. But for as sexy as he was, he was a billionaire. In the same class with Greg. Combine sexy and billionaire and the self-protection instincts she should have had with Riley's dad came popping out.

She sighed. "I'm sorry. I'm short. I'm blond.

Everybody thinks I need a keeper. My motto is never show weakness."

He chuckled. "You are anything but weak. In fact, your strength is part of what makes you so intriguing."

She felt herself blushing. Men found her formidable, sexy, even a challenge. But no one ever said she was intriguing and damned if that didn't please her a little too much.

She reminded herself that he was in Greg's world, not hers, but even if he wasn't there were plenty of other reasons she couldn't get involved with him. "You know my story. People disappointed me. I had to become strong."

He picked up one of the menus sitting on the table and began perusing it. "I get it. But I'm still sending a limo for you tonight for the dinner you promised GiGi you'd have with us."

His tight tone made her feel a little silly for reminding him she was strong. "I apologize again. I think deciding to spend two weeks planning the wedding has me all wound up and I'm even more feisty than I usually am."

"Feisty." He pondered the word. "I like that."

"I've been told more than once I can be overassertive."

"Honestly? You being you doesn't bother me. After a few decades of running a business, I learned a lot about the importance of getting to know the real person...not the facade they present."

She leaned toward him conspiratorially. "I know! It's amazing how many people are fakes, isn't it?"

"It was the first thing I taught Antonio." He snorted. "The boy is good-looking, rich and smart. I didn't want him to be taken in by someone with a smooth line. Yet he made the same mistake I did and married a trophy wife, who took him for a bundle when he divorced her."

"Riley lived with three guys who weren't right for her."

The server arrived and poured coffee before she wrote down their breakfast orders.

When she walked away, Lorenzo said, "It took a while for me to realize Antonio didn't learn from my mistake because I protected him from his mother."

"Protected him?"

"I was careful about his visits with her when he was a child and even more careful when he became a teenager. His mom was such a party girl that I worried she'd introduce him to more than wine."

Julie gasped. "Oh, my goodness!"

"I did a lot of worrying and watching. Luckily, Antonio was basically a good kid. Head down in school, working toward good grades, knowing the family business would be his responsibility someday."

She nodded.

"Then there's GiGi and her love of people. She's let many a stranger spend weeks at the villa." He shook his head. "I love her kindness when someone needs a helping hand. But she can't seem to separate the needy from the grifters."

"She has a good heart."

"Yes. And she has me to make sure she doesn't run into trouble with any of her rescues."

From the way Riley had talked, Juliette had believed GiGi was the head of the family, but ten minutes of conversation showed her Lorenzo was. GiGi might rule like a queen, but Lorenzo was the person in the background who saw everything and kept their lives on track. It was equal parts of sexy and confusing. She did not like anyone telling her what to do, yet being the boss was clearly part of his personality.

"I had to gently guide Riley about the first couple of people she hired. She loves everyone too. But every person a manager hires has to be able to do the job. I was lucky that she appreciated my advice."

"It sounds like we're two peas in a pod."

It did…but they weren't. She might have a good life, but he had wealth, power and status beyond what she'd ever know.

She pulled back. "I think you and I are very different."

He laughed. "I have more money, maybe. But you're doing okay."

She nodded. "I am. In fact, I'm doing very well. I came from nothing and became something. I'm a bit of a scrapper."

He chuckled. "Are you telling me that a junkyard dog will beat the purebred?"

"No. Because we're not fighting."

He chuckled softly. "Establishing ground rules, then?"

"Maybe." She'd made the mistake of thinking the differences in her background and Greg's meant nothing. Older, wiser, she knew they had. And that was an error she would not repeat.

The server arrived with their breakfast, and their conversation stopped except for a few comments about their food and the weather. As they finished eating, a tall, dark-haired gentleman walked up to their table.

Lorenzo rose. "Marco! I didn't expect to see you this morning. I thought you had breakfast with another supplier."

He said, "I did. But I spoke with Antonio and he told me you were having breakfast with Riley's mom." He faced Juliette. "You do not look old enough to have a daughter Riley's age."

She laughed at the flattery. She didn't know

who this guy was, but he was as smooth as Lorenzo. "I can assure you I am Riley's mom."

"Juliette, this is my *former* friend Marco."

Marco chortled as he faced Lorenzo. "After my meeting, I tried to call you to see if I could get a ride to your office with you. When you didn't answer your phone, I called your house."

Lorenzo winced. "I turned my phone off."

"I see why."

Ignoring the comment, Lorenzo glanced at Juliette. "You are fine on your own this morning?"

Knowing he was only asking out of politeness, not because he thought she was helpless, she picked up her purse and started to rise. "Absolutely."

Marco offered a hand to help her. She took it with a smile. The way Lorenzo's face contorted surprised her, but she ignored it. She had to arrange to go home the next day and should make notes about what things needed to be done while she would be in Italy. She'd be too busy to need a tour guide or someone to eat lunch with.

Which was good. She might have decided he had to be off-limits because he was too much like Greg, but she couldn't talk herself out of being attracted to him.

Still, that was a problem for later. She was a strong enough woman that she could behave so well not one person would even guess she was attracted to him.

"Gentlemen. If you'll excuse me."

Marco gallantly said, "Of course," and let her pass.

Lorenzo said nothing until she was out of sight then he turned on Marco. "What are you doing? I called your office to let you know I wouldn't see you until this afternoon."

Marco shrugged. "Didn't get the message. Besides, some of what we have to do today can't wait till this afternoon."

Lorenzo took a long breath and headed out the door. "You could have told my staff that. Not let me think you'd barged in on our breakfast to meet Juliette."

"What would have been the fun in that?"

His suspicions tripled. "You *did* want to see Juliette!"

He shrugged. "So? You said yourself you aren't interested."

"There's enough stress in this family right now without you playing Romeo."

"I wouldn't play Romeo! I would *be* Romeo."

Lorenzo rolled his eyes. "She wouldn't fall for that."

"Really? Maybe we will see?"

Jealousy set his blood on fire, but he stopped

it because Juliette was leaving the next day and Marco would be back in Paris before she returned. The chances of them running into each other again were small.

They walked outside and got into Lorenzo's limo. Marco immediately began discussing business, but Lorenzo only half listened. He wasn't jealous. He really did want Marco to stay out of the picture to prevent even more drama in his family, but damned if it didn't rub him the wrong way that Marco was interested in Juliette.

He tried to comfort himself with the knowledge that anybody would be interested in Juliette. She wasn't just gorgeous. She was smart and strong. As he'd told her, she was intriguing.

And she was the perfect age. They had similar life experiences. He and Juliette could talk honestly and understand each other's perspective—

That was the problem. He wasn't merely attracted to her. He saw something *more* in her. Not just a few dates or an affair…but *more*.

The thought shook him to his core. The guy who'd lived through the marriage from hell was thinking about *more*?

It was foolishness. He had learned his lesson about *more*. If his interest in Juliette went beyond a couple of months of being together for fun, then anything romantic between them really was wrong.

Fun? Fling? Romance? All fine.

Commitment? Seeing her as something more? *Wrong*.

His feelings for Juliette sorted, he forced his attention to what Marco was saying. From here on out, he would redirect conversations with her to the wedding. No more personal chitchat.

When the limo arrived to pick her up that night, Lorenzo was in it. Juliette almost made a comment about how they seemed to spend a lot of time in the back of a car like two teenagers but wasn't sure he'd get the reference. And, if he did, it might not be smart to think about that.

"How was your day?"

She leaned back against the seat. The intimacy of the space instantly reminded her of how attracted she was to the man sitting next to her, but she didn't let it show. When it came to controlling her emotions, she could have the strength of Hercules.

"I spent it going through digital files and making lists of things I need to discuss with Pete, my second in command, when I get back to the office. I won't leave any stone unturned."

He laughed. "The things we do for our kids."

She snorted. "Tell me about it."

"You really are okay with this wedding?"

"I just needed to remember that my daughter doesn't do anything rashly. I trust her."

"I trust Antonio too."

"They might end up being the happiest two people in the world."

He laughed. "Because they are acting on instinct."

His beautiful accent sent warmth shimmying through her. The instincts it inspired were every bit as tempting as what Antonio and Riley were feeling. Again, she controlled it. Especially when a quick peek at Lorenzo revealed nothing. She might be feeling things, but he was fine.

"Not all instincts are supposed to be followed through on."

"Yes."

The back seat got quiet. The scent of his aftershave drifted to her, and she stifled a sigh. This wasn't a fair fight. He was gorgeous. He smelled great. His accent could charm the angels and he wasn't a bossy, jump-to-conclusions person. He thought about other people. Wanted to see everyone happy. But while he liked her feistiness, he seemed to not be fighting the same attraction she was. Which was a relief. Really. Knowing his attraction to her was dimming as they spent time together would help her stay in line.

The limo stopped in front of the villa. Lorenzo exited and helped Juliette out. They walked into the foyer and were greeted by a gentleman who took their coats.

Lorenzo's head tilted when he saw her pretty blue dress. "You look lovely."

After how neutral he'd been in the limo, she took the compliment as merely a polite acknowledgement from a gentleman. "The way your mother talked, I got the sense that your dinners are semi-formal."

He shrugged. "Sometimes."

"Is tonight one of those times?"

He put his hand on the small of her back to direct her into the living room. "Probably."

She laughed, but with his hand on her back, the sound was strained. Everything about him appealed to her. But he no longer seemed interested.

Because they had kids who were getting married.

Not only did he not want to do anything to jeopardize the fragile peace they'd finally found about the wedding, but they would be connected for years after the wedding. If they started something that ended badly, every holiday would be strained. They couldn't risk it.

He'd said it and now he was behaving appropriately.

It made perfect sense and she would work harder to do the same.

GiGi rose when they entered the room. She wore a scarf over her head that matched her simple green dress. She appeared tired, as if her chemo treatments were wearing her out. When Juliette reached her, she caught both of her hands. "How kind of you to join us."

"Your invitation was kind."

Motioning for Juliette to sit beside her on the sofa, GiGi said, "I understand you're going home for a few days then coming back for two weeks for wedding planning."

"Yes," Juliette said. "I'm very excited."

"So is Riley. She's put everything on hold until you get here." She squeezed Juliette's hands. "I'm so glad you will be staying with us!"

The future bride and groom entered from a doorway in the back. Both were grinning. Antonio said, "Good evening, everyone."

GiGi said, "Antonio! Riley!"

Lorenzo walked to the bar. "Who wants a drink?"

He filled beautiful crystal glasses with white wine and distributed them, then he sat on the big chair on the right of the sofa. Antonio sat on the big chair to the left, with Riley sitting on the chair's wide arm, as if she loved being close to her new fiancé.

Another layer of peace filled Juliette. There

wasn't a ripple of discontent. No disturbance in the air. She'd never seen Riley so happy.

The doorbell rang. Not one person in the living room even blinked, as someone from their staff answered it.

After a few seconds, Marco walked in.

Antonio said, "Marco! Thank you for joining us."

Marco grinned. "Thank you for inviting me."

GiGi and Lorenzo rose. GiGi clasped his fingers the same way she had Juliette's. "It is wonderful to see you."

Lorenzo shook his hand. "Yes. *Wonderful.*"

Juliette glanced from one man to the other. Marco looked like a guy who'd pulled off a great coup. Lorenzo looked like someone had stolen his lunch.

Marco headed for the sofa. "Juliette! Lovely to see you!"

Just when Marco would have sat beside her on the sofa, Lorenzo intercepted him. "Please. You're a guest. Take the chair." He pointed at the chair he'd been sitting in and blocked the way to the sofa.

Marco paused. Juliette swore he was about to argue, then he smiled broadly and said, "Thank you."

He sat on the chair. Lorenzo sat beside Juliette on the sofa.

She peeked at him from her peripheral vision. He'd clearly not wanted Marco to sit on the sofa—

A laugh bubbled up and she swallowed it.

He was jealous.

All this time she'd been so worried about controlling her own feelings, she hadn't seen his weren't as simple and handled as he'd tried to make her think.

Then Marco had shown up.

And calm, cool, collected Lorenzo was jealous.

CHAPTER FIVE

HE WAS NOT JEALOUS.

Lorenzo told himself that as they ate dinner. He reminded himself of that when they sat in the living room with dessert.

When everyone was finished, Antonio and Riley excused themselves. They had plans with another couple in town.

After they exited, Marco rose. "This has been wonderful," he said to GiGi. "But I need to get back to my hotel." He faced Juliette. "We're staying at the same place. Shall we ride together this time?"

Lorenzo's nerves crackled. They shouldn't have. Not only had he decided that he and Juliette couldn't be romantically involved, but also it made sense for Marco and Juliette to leave at the same time and share the limo. Plus, there was no reason for him to ride into town again, except he liked Juliette's company—

And that was dangerous territory. Something he should be avoiding.

Still, he didn't like the idea of Marco romancing her. She was a good person who'd been hurt once. Marco could hurt her again. God only knew what could happen in the darkness and privacy of the back of the limo—

Oh, Lord. Why had he let himself think about the darkness and privacy of the back seat of a limo? He knew exactly what could happen!

She started to rise. His nerve endings renewed their crackle—

But GiGi stopped her. "Stay a bit, Juliette." She caught Lorenzo's gaze. "You too." Then she rose and walked over to hug Marco. "It was lovely seeing you."

He kissed both her cheeks. "You too, GiGi."

He faced Juliette. "Maybe you and I can have breakfast tomorrow?"

"She's leaving early tomorrow." The words were out of Lorenzo's mouth before he even thought about them. But they were true. She was leaving town. She'd be back in a few days but there was no reason for Marco to know that.

Marco inclined his head. "Then I'll say goodnight."

He left the room, and silence hung in the air like a cloud of doom. He wasn't sure what his mother wanted to discuss with him and Juliette, but she rarely asked for privacy.

She took the big chair and motioned for them

to sit across from her on the sofa. They sat simultaneously like two bad kids who'd been sent to the headmaster's office.

"Juliette, I'm so happy that you are going to be spending time in the villa."

Juliette smiled. Lorenzo sat back on the sofa. Juliette had told him she'd be staying at the villa, but that fact suddenly hit him full force. He would see her breakfast, lunch and dinner. Of course, he could spend a lot of time in his office and if need be he could hide out in the den. But he wasn't a coward. Surely, he could get control of his attraction to her.

"There are many things we have to plan for the wedding."

GiGi said, "*Sì*. But I also want this time to get to know you. We'll be spending a lot of time together over the years."

"Yes. We will."

"I want you to be comfortable in our home. I almost feel like we should dedicate a suite to you so that you will know you are always welcome anytime."

"You are extremely kind. But I don't want you to go out of your way for me."

"It is no trouble. Though I'm sure you'll want Riley and Antonio to visit you in Manhattan—especially once the grandkids arrive—holidays might be easier here."

Juliette nodded. "It would be simpler for me to fly here than it would be for Antonio and Riley to pack up kids and Christmas gifts and whatever else just to even the score about who visits when."

Lorenzo glanced at her in surprise. When she said she thought something through, she thought it through the whole way. And extremely honestly. Selflessly. She could be arguing to get at least one holiday in her home. Instead, she thought of Riley and Antonio and their future kids.

Something his ex would have never done.

GiGi said, "Which is why I think assigning one of our suites to you permanently might make the whole transition easier."

Juliette hesitated, then she inclined her head. "It might. But the truth is everything is happening so fast that I feel like maybe we should just let some things work themselves out."

GiGi laughed. "I'm an old woman who has very happily gotten new life in her home again. I want everyone to be happy with what we decide."

Lorenzo said, "We will be. But I think Juliette's correct. We have so much to do with the wedding that we can figure the other things out later."

"Okay." GiGi agreed but she sighed and rose. "Sometimes I know I fuss too much. But it gives me great joy to have a future with my family again. Now, if you'll excuse me, I've worn myself out today."

Lorenzo kissed his mother's cheek before she walked out of the room and to the elevator that would take her to her second-floor suite. When she was gone, he faced Juliette. "I hope she didn't offend you."

"I hope I didn't offend her, but you have to admit things are happening so fast we're getting ahead of ourselves."

"Yes and no. You have an uncanny ability to put us back on track."

"Right. Yesterday, I got overwhelmed. Today, I nixed the idea of getting a permanent suite in your house when GiGi might be right. But it just seems off to be planning the next twenty years of our lives."

"GiGi isn't planning twenty years. I think she simply wants everything settled so she can enjoy it in the last years she has left." He laughed. "Besides, there are people who would pay good money for a permanent suite here."

"I'm sure." She rose with a sigh as GiGi had. "Honestly, it's been such a long day and tomorrow I'm flying out again. I should get back to the hotel."

He stood up too. "Okay."

Juliette headed for the foyer, and he walked

out after her. He took her coat from the butler and helped her slide into it.

She faced him with a smile. "I'll see you when I return?"

"Actually, you're not done seeing me today."

She smiled slyly. "Are you afraid of me being alone with the limo driver?"

Oh, Lord. She hadn't missed his maneuvering with Marco. "No. Marco took the limo. I'll be driving you back to the hotel."

Juliette blinked. She hadn't thought anything of it when Marco left, but even if the Salvaggios had an extra limo, there probably wasn't a second driver on duty.

Lorenzo led her to a huge garage to the right of the house. They walked in through a side door, and he hit a button that caused a cascade of lights until the entire garage was lit. Unlike the garages she'd seen in her neighborhood when she was a kid, this one was open. Cars weren't parked in a straight line. They were angled as if they were being displayed.

And why not? She saw a Bentley, an Aston Martin, four sports cars she couldn't name, and various SUVs and sedans, probably for everyday use.

"Holy cow!"

"You've never seen a garage before?"

"I've never known anyone who owned…" She paused to count. "Fifteen cars."

"Antonio is the car guy. Now that I've done with my years of speeding on the A1, I'm happy with a limo and an SUV." He motioned around the room. "What's your pleasure?"

She didn't even hesitate. "I love the Aston Martin."

He walked to the back, where he used a keypad to unlock a room. A few seconds later he emerged with the car starter. He opened the passenger door for her and scooted around the front to get behind the wheel.

She caressed the leather. "This is beautiful!"

He laughed. "We like it."

He started the car and drove to a garage door that opened automatically as he approached, then they headed out into the night. Accustomed to city lights, she was amazed at how dark it was when they reached the country road.

The beautiful night and beautiful car were so romantic that she struggled with her attraction again. After short stretches of time with his family, they always seemed to end up alone. But the chat with GiGi reinforced what they both already knew. They would be together, as family, forever now. A romance between them was out of the question.

The car sputtered oddly. Lorenzo muttered,

"What the heck?" Then he looked down at the console and sighed. "Antonio and Riley must have taken this car out for their errands today."

He turned the vehicle to the side of the road. The car sputtered some more then slowed to a stop on the berm.

Lorenzo faced her. "We're out of petrol."

"Well, that's not good."

"We're not even a mile from the house." He opened his car door. "Consider it a stroll in the moonlight."

He closed his door and disappeared into the darkness. Juliette opened her door and found him walking around the back of the car, on his way to help her out. She displayed her pale blue high heels. "These aren't walking shoes, buddy."

He took her hand, nudging her out of the car. "Don't tell me you've never spent a day running around Manhattan in those beauties."

She scowled. "I have. But it's not the same as walking on the side of the road."

"You can walk on the road. Pretend it's a sidewalk."

She sighed and they made their way to the pavement. She could feel the shale and dry dirt taking chips out of her pretty blue shoes. But she didn't say a word or even sigh. Things like cars running out of gas happened.

"I never even thought to check the gauge."

"Because you have staff who does that?"

"Well, yes."

His billionaire mindset sent another ripple of warning through her. He could be so open and congenial that she sometimes forgot how wealthy and pampered he was. How different his life was from hers.

He sighed. "I'm guessing Antonio and Riley returned after the maintenance guy went home for the day. He probably would have filled the tank first thing in the morning."

She glanced up at the wide-open sky. The stars were bright. The crescent moon looked like a shiny sliver of glass. He might be pampered but she wasn't. Pretty shoes or not, she wasn't afraid of a little walk, especially on such a beautiful night. "The sky is so clear."

He peeked up. "I know."

She took a long breath of the air that held the scent of the soil and the plants it nurtured. It was all amazing, but it was also dark. So dark she could barely see where they were going.

Half of her was tempted to nestle against him. Now that the thrill of the beauty of her surroundings was gone, her courage began to desert her, and she started to wonder if Italy had bears…or wolves…or snakes. Did snakes sleep at night? Or did they prowl?

She shuddered.

"Are you cold?"

"No. Letting my imagination run wild. You don't have bears or wolves around here, do you?"

He laughed. "You really are a city girl."

She lifted her chin. "Nothing wrong with that."

"Nothing at all," he agreed with a chuckle. "I love Manhattan and I like your city-girl sophistication."

"Okay. Let's see. You find me intriguing. You like my sophistication. You like that I'm feisty. Anything else I should know?"

"I wanted to ask Marco to shut up and stop stealing all your attention at dinner."

She laughed. "I picked up on that."

He snorted but said nothing and she winced. GiGi wanting to assign a suite to her really had brought home how connected she and Lorenzo would be in the future. If he was fighting the same attraction she was, this was something they needed to discuss.

"Don't clam up now."

"Why not?"

"Because we need to talk about this. Marco monopolizing the conversation annoyed you because you were jealous, and it might be smart if we got it out in the open so we could deal with it."

"Deal with me being jealous?"

"In a way, we've already sorted all this. We're not good for each other. Our kids are getting married. Our lives will be connected forever. If we give in to our attraction, then every holiday, baby baptism and birthday could be awkward. GiGi wanting to give me a permanent suite in your house really brought that home for me."

"Which makes me right. It's pointless to talk about the fact that I'm so ridiculously interested in you that I got jealous."

She casually said, "Yeah," but the feeling racing through her wasn't as simple as agreement that he was correct, or disappointment that they were wrong for each other, or even flightiness like the sense of destiny she'd had about him when she first met him. The feeling that lodged in the pit of her stomach was somehow different. The sense that being logical was the wrong move here.

He took her hand in the darkness. "This isn't a pass. This is for guidance. It's dark out here."

His hand felt so good wrapped around hers. "And there might be bears."

Even as she said that, her foot missed the pavement and fell another three inches to the dirt. Her ankle gave, but so did her heel. When she heard a slight snap, she prayed it was her shoe.

She stopped.

"What's up?"

"I either broke my ankle or my shoe."

"If it was your ankle you'd be crying."

He stooped down, took her foot in his hands. The way he gently turned it from side to side almost felt like a caress.

Tingles of arousal formed where pain should have been. Her ankle definitely wasn't broken.

"It's your shoe. You no longer have a heel on your high heel."

She swallowed, almost willing him to slide his hand from her ankle up her calf. It felt so wonderful to have him touch her.

But it was wrong. It had to be wrong. Babies, baptisms, birthdays had to be considered. Plus, they were worlds apart as she and Greg had been. And she knew how that ended.

She swallowed again. "So, my shoe is broken?"

"Yep. The good news is you can see the villa lights from here. I told you we hadn't even gone a mile."

"Well, the bad news is my hobbling on one shoe will slow us down."

He laughed. "I could always put you on my back. Like the piggyback rides I used to give Antonio when he was a toddler."

She sighed. With the way her thoughts kept going back and forth it was not wise for her to be that close to him. "Or I could take my other shoe off and walk barefoot."

"It's cold."

She rubbed her arms. "I know. And the longer we stand out here talking about it, the colder it gets."

He lifted her second foot and removed the other shoe. "Okay, but if you change your mind—"

She laughed. "I won't." She couldn't. His being jealous had tickled her a little too much. Still, she could talk herself out of that. She could also keep the attraction at bay by sheer force of will. But she wouldn't tempt fate by putting them into any closer proximity than they already were.

They walked a bit with her feet feeling both the cold and the stones. The lights of the villa buildings got closer and closer but when they reached the lane to the house, she realized they weren't actually home yet. There was at least a quarter mile to walk down the long lane to the house.

He paused. "Okay. We're done with you showing me how tough you are." He presented his back. "Hop on."

She sucked in a breath. With freezing feet that had been bitten up by stones, she couldn't argue. She walked over. Balancing her hands on his shoulders, she hiked first one knee against his side, then the other.

He handed her shoes to her then put his hands beneath her butt and hoisted her up higher. "You settled?"

She burst out laughing to hide the sizzle of attraction that zipped through her. "Yes."

"Do you want me to whinny or snort or something? Antonio seemed to particularly enjoy that when he was four."

She laughed again. "No. Let's just get back to your house."

But the temptation arose to snuggle against his back, nuzzle her nose in his shaggy hair, sniff his aftershave. Just the thought tightened her chest, so she stopped herself, keeping herself a few inches away from nestling against him— or even leaning against him.

She couldn't even imagine what he was feeling with her thighs against his sides and her dress riding up almost to her hips.

There simply was no graceful way to ride piggyback.

Two steps before they would have turned to walk down the lane, car lights approached, illuminating their path as the vehicle drove by.

"Well, that's about ten minutes too late."

Juliette said, "Yeah. Are you sure you're okay carrying me? I could probably tough out the walk down the lane."

"I'm fine. You're not exactly heavy."

Right in that moment she thanked her lucky stars that she worked out regularly and rarely indulged in the doughnuts Riley liked so much.

As she'd assumed, the remainder of the walk took fifteen minutes. Fifteen long minutes of temptation. Especially after the scent of him wafted to her naturally. It seemed a shame that they were from such different worlds and also had a future of potentially awkward holidays to consider.

When they reached the stairs to the stoop in front of the door, he slid her down and punched in a code to open it. She eased her scrunched dress down her thighs and desperately tried to regain her dignity as she forced herself to forget the feeling of being so close to him.

He opened the door and she gingerly walked inside, removing her coat and hanging it on the newel post of the stairway. "My feet are probably filthy. Can you get me a cloth or a towel, so I don't leave footprints all over the place?"

He laughed and walked away, returning with a wet cloth and a dry one. Then he headed for the sitting room. "I don't know about you. But I think this calls for bourbon."

She finished wiping her feet. Whether he was tired from carrying her or as flummoxed by their proximity as she was, it didn't matter. A drink was definitely in order. "I think it calls for bourbon too."

She walked into the room to find he'd lit a fire in the stone fireplace. The warmth of it reminded her how cold she was. She padded over to him. He handed her drink to her. "Thanks."

The fire illuminated the small section in front of the sofa. They sat and she sighed with relief.

He took a sip of his bourbon, then sighed too. "What a night."

She laughed. "I know."

He pulled a throw from the back of the sofa and tucked it around her, leaving the hand holding her drink free. "I don't think you and I have ever had a normal time together."

She snuggled into the throw. "Breakfast the day I got here was pretty normal."

"You mean the day we were talking about our evil plan?"

She laughed.

"I hate to tell you this, but that's not normal."

He lifted the corner of the throw and eased under with her. "You know, things like this aren't supposed to happen to suave rich guys."

"So I've heard."

He leaned against her, sharing her warmth. "But maybe this is part of what makes you so intriguing."

She almost snorted bourbon through her nose.

"Usually when a guy tells a woman she's intriguing it means she's stunning, sleek, sophisticated. Not trouble."

"Oh, I don't know. Sometimes trouble's fun."

She glanced at the elegant, controlled guy beside her. "Were you ever really in trouble?"

He shrugged. "All kids push a boundary or two." He glanced over at her. "I'll bet you did."

"Believe it or not, I didn't. Being on my own after my parents died, I couldn't. And I stayed that way. I don't throw temper tantrums or complain out loud."

"Just in your head."

"Just in my head."

"That doesn't give a guy a chance to argue his case."

She pondered that. "Never thought of it that way."

"What else don't you do in Manhattan?"

"Walk barefoot. Anywhere. Ever."

He gasped. "That's a shame. There's nothing like the feeling of soft grass under your feet."

"I sort of remember from my childhood." She took a drink of her whiskey, then sighed. "Anyway, as much as I'd love to just sit here and watch the fire, I need to get back to the hotel."

"Why don't you stay tonight?"

She slowly turned her head to look at him. He was such an open, honest person she couldn't believe he was hinting at something. But she didn't know him well enough to assume he wasn't. "You're not asking what it sounds like you're asking, are you?"

"I wish I could. But we both know anything between us is a potential landmine in the future. That means we're not looking at this as just fun. We both know there could be something more and we both know that doesn't work for us. Otherwise, we wouldn't care. We'd jump into bed and never think of it again—except fondly."

She laughed, but the truth of that rumbled through her. She might have thought the similarities between his life and Greg's were what bothered her, but that wouldn't matter if she was simply thinking about an affair. Just like him, she realized there could be something more between them. And *that* was where the trouble lay.

"Yeah. I get it."

He thought for a second, then said, "All that is true, but you know what? I don't think it's fair that we never even get to kiss, to get a taste of what we're missing."

With him so close, the heat of him keeping them both cozy and warm, it did seem a shame that they'd never kiss.

She set her bourbon on the coffee table and leaned toward him. He leaned toward her. Their mouths met softly, chastely, then he pulled away.

She caught his shoulders and brought him back. That was not the way he wanted to kiss her or she wanted to kiss him. She opened her mouth over his and after a quick second of shock, he put himself into the kiss.

Tingles of arousal poured through her. She slid her hands up his shoulders to his nape to feel his hair. He deepened the kiss again, his tongue sliding across hers, raising goose bumps. She wiggled closer, pressing against him, making herself sigh with pleasure. If they ever got the chance to make love, she would drown in him.

The thought brought her back to her senses. She pulled away and they stared at each other.

Then he smiled sexily. "I knew it would be worth it."

That brought her out of her haze. If she stayed another ten minutes with this guy, under this blanket, they'd end up doing things they'd agreed they weren't going to do. Gloriously seductive, his kiss had drawn her into a place she hadn't been in decades. She'd felt the sweet sensation of connection, along with that cursed feeling of destiny.

The connection she could deal with. That sense of destiny was nothing but trouble. He might like trouble, but she didn't.

She rose from the sofa. "Let's get me to the hotel."

He groaned. "Really?"

She busied herself picking up the throw they'd snuggled under and neatly folding it. "Yes. I have a plane to catch tomorrow."

He gave her a confused look. "You're ending our night when it feels like we're just getting started?"

"You're incorrigible." She marched to the foyer where she found her coat and shoes but only one was wearable.

He leaned against the doorway. "You're going to have to walk into a lobby, past a noisy bar, with only one shoe."

She sucked in a breath. "Better late at night than in the morning when people are sober and wide awake."

He laughed. "Perhaps. But let me suggest that you stay overnight and tomorrow you can borrow a pair of your daughter's shoes. We can put you in a suite and call it yours permanently, the way GiGi wanted."

She sighed. "I really do need to get back to the hotel. I haven't even changed my flight yet. Then I'd like to get at least a little sleep, so I don't arrive in Manhattan like a zombie."

"Okay. But you wait here. Let me get the car."

"All right."

He arrived a few minutes later with a big black

SUV. She raced outside and opened the door before he could.

By the time they reached her hotel, she'd decided to toss her shoes in the trash, so she didn't have to carry them—all but suggesting people look at her feet—as she walked through the lobby without shoes.

He laughed as he parked the car. "At least let me walk in with you so your bare feet aren't so obvious."

"You think people won't notice I'm barefoot if I walk in with you?"

"I think people won't care that you're without shoes. They'll look at us, wonder what we're doing in a hotel, wonder if we're married, or having an affair."

She laughed and shook her head. He was probably right. "Whatever."

They walked into the hotel and through the lobby as if nothing was amiss. She knew people noticed them. She knew they wondered who they were just as Lorenzo had suggested.

When they got to the elevator, she giggled. "That was sort of fun."

"Affairs with me are *always* fun."

She didn't doubt it for one second.

He pressed the button for the elevator. The doors opened slowly. She started inside. "Thanks for dinner, the ride to town and mostly for the piggyback ride."

He laughed, caught her hand and pulled her out of the elevator again. Before she could stop him, he kissed her deeply, then looked into her eyes.

"I want you to dream about me tonight."

She walked into the elevator shakily. Good grief! Either he was the most suave, sexy guy in the world…or he had some of the best lines.

The doors began to close. He smiled at her.

She stared at him. When the two panels met fully, she blew her breath out on a long sigh.

Wow. Just wow. She hadn't had feelings like these *ever* in her life. She'd thought falling for Greg was romantic and it had been. But this was beyond that. Warm. Tingly. And connected. There was something wonderful about being with him. Almost like they understood each other. And maybe they did? They were well versed in the game of life. They knew the realities of sex and relationships. And they still wanted it.

They both wanted it. Each could feel that coming from the other. She couldn't hide it any more than he could.

But it was a complication. Their lives were such that they couldn't have anything but an affair. They couldn't "date." Whatever they had would lead nowhere. So…

They would have to have a secret affair. That way there would be no mess when they broke up and still had to see each other for their grand-children's baptisms and birthdays—

After the thrill of the short walk to the eleva-tor, a secret affair didn't merely seem possible… it felt romantic. And after that kiss she wasn't sure if her thinking was correct or if a secret affair simply felt so right that she wasn't think-ing at all.

Which made it good that she was going home. She'd be back in a few days to spend two weeks at the Salvaggio villa and the temptation would be overwhelming. She definitely needed some distance to clear her head.

They both had to be on the same page. Secret affair. No talk of the future. Just fun for how-ever long it lasted.

If they didn't agree, then they had to be adults and stop flirting.

She laughed. She wasn't entirely sure Lorenzo knew how to stop flirting. But she did. Sexy or not, he wasn't irresistible… He was close. But she was the one who had taught Riley had to be a strong, smart woman.

She could handle this.

Though it was late, she called the airline and changed her ticket before she showered and packed to return to Manhattan. She woke early, dressed and headed out. If she hurried, she had just enough time to get to the airport, check in and grab a bagel at a coffee shop in the terminal.

Happy with her plan, she rolled her suitcase to the door and opened it. A box fell into her room. Confused, she bent down and picked it up. A note was taped to it.

I couldn't find a shoemaker to fix your heel, but my assistant did find these this morning.

She opened the box and found a pair of blue shoes identical to the ones she'd broken the night before.

She laughed out loud, then packed the shoes in her suitcase and left her room to check out. It was definitely time to leave. The man could charm the birds from the trees. At home, she would develop a plan to resist him.

CHAPTER SIX

SATURDAY MORNING, Lorenzo woke knowing he wouldn't see Juliette that day. She was returning to New York, but when she came back to Italy, it would be for two weeks—

And she'd be living in his house.

Decisions needed to be made before then So maybe it was a good thing she'd left for a while. These days apart gave them a cooling off period. The next time they saw each other, their kisses wouldn't be so fresh in their minds, and they could behave like adults about it.

Which was wise.

Smart.

Because getting involved with each other might not be the good idea he had thought it to be the night before when they were snuggled under the blanket. In the light of day, he remembered that they had babies and birthdays and holidays to consider. No one wanted things to be awkward between them, ruining festive events for everyone. Especially not him. Or Juliette. She'd said no at least three times the night before, when he would have thrown caution to the wind.

As much as he liked her, an affair between them clearly wasn't a good idea.

He pondered that as he was driven to work to catch up on things best handled on Saturday morning when his office was quiet. The limo now reminded him of Juliette. Reminded him of how sassy and funny she could be. Reminded him that in a world of people who wanted something from him, she didn't give a damn who he was. She spoke her mind.

Sleeping with her would probably be as honest and real as it was fun.

To get those vivid images out of his brain, he read contracts all morning and by noon he was exhausted and sick of legalese. After lunch with GiGi, he went to the den where he found a sporting event on the television and relaxed in a recliner to watch it.

Just when he was getting into the game, Antonio walked in. "Funny thing."

Lorenzo sat up. "What?"

"Gino told me you sent him down the road this morning to get the Aston Martin."

"Because you used all the petrol, and the car conked out when I was driving Juliette back to her hotel. It was no big deal."

Antonio flopped on a chair. "Gino said it was

over half a mile down the road. How'd you get back to the villa in the dark?"

"Walked."

"You walked?"

"Yes."

"Interesting."

He gaped at his son. "Why is that interesting?"

"Because one of the staff said they heard someone say that they'd seen someone walking along our road with a woman on his back."

He sputtered upright. "The heel broke off her shoe! And since when do you listen to someone who says they heard someone who heard someone else say something? That's usually gossip."

"But you admitted it."

"Okay. This time it wasn't gossip. But I taught you better than to listen to rumors."

Antonio laughed heartily. "I'd have paid to see that. You're both such sticks in the mud—"

Righteous indignation roared through Lorenzo. "I'm not a stick in the mud!"

His son batted a hand. "I don't remember the last time you did something foolish."

"It's called being an adult."

Antonio took the remote and focused his attention on the TV. "Whatever."

He said it simply, ending the conversation and the teasing, but a sharp jab of reality stabbed through Lorenzo. His life had gotten predictable and boring. Now fate had sent Juliette to him, and he was arguing?

He pulled in a breath, pretending to fix his attention on the TV again, but Antonio was too damned right for him to focus. Where was his spunk? His fire? He was wild about Juliette and lusting after her like a schoolboy. Not so long ago, he wouldn't have talked it to death. He simply would have initiated an affair. After what would undoubtedly be the best sex of his life, he would have reminded her it would be prudent to keep their relationship to themselves. Because if no one knew they were sleeping together, then no one would be awkward at birthdays and baptisms and whatever the hell else they would do together.

The only two people who would know if they were sleeping together or had broken up would be him and Juliette. And they'd already proven they could keep a secret—

And be mature after a breakup. Despite his horrible marriage, he never spoke unkindly about his ex for Antonio's sake. And despite her horrible situation with Riley's father, Juliette didn't speak ill of him.

They were the perfect candidates for an affair.

Sunday at noon, Juliette's phone rang just as she was struggling with her takeout lunch, her briefcase and the key to unlock her front door. Traveling the day before had been exhausting enough that she'd spent what was left of Saturday recovering from jet lag. But that morning she'd called Pete, her second in command, and arranged to meet him at the office to begin sorting through the work he would be handling for the next two weeks. In four hours, they had put a significant dent in the projects he would oversee while she was gone. But, not wanting to overwhelm him, she'd stopped at noon, then gone to a deli for a good salad because she was starving. Whoever was calling they were going to have to wait.

The lock gave and she entered her condo, racing the distance to her kitchen island to rid herself of the salad and briefcase.

Out of breath, she rummaged through her purse for her phone and answered, "Hello?"

Lorenzo's laugh drifted to her. "Working? On a Sunday? We *are* the two most boring people in the world."

Her heart stuttered. She hadn't thought she would miss him—or that beautiful voice—but the sound of it filled her with pleasure. "You know I had to come home to prep Pete to work without me for two weeks."

She slid out of her coat, then curled up on her sofa, her toes under her butt. Just hearing his voice had zapped her tiredness and while she should probably be careful about that, she needed this break.

"Exactly. That's boring."

"Oh, yeah. What did you do today?"

"Today is my second day of reading contracts."

"Ugh! And you called me boring! There is nothing more boring in the world than reading contracts." She paused only a second, then said, "So what's up? Nothing wrong with the kids, is there?"

"No. They're still gloriously happy and looking forward to your arrival."

"I thought they'd be wedding planning."

"No one is even talking about it. Riley said she wants you in on all that fun, so no one is even permitted to mention a potential appetizer."

She laughed.

"You really do have a good relationship with her."

"And you have a good relationship with Antonio."

He paused. His voice was cautious when he said, "That sort of brings me to the reason I called."

"The fact that we're good parents?"

"Yes. We're such good parents that we want to do all the right things for our kids. But I think denying ourselves the pleasure of an affair goes above and beyond what good parents would do."

Her heart rate plunged then shot up again. "You think we should have an affair?" The memory of their kisses flashed through her brain and her chest tightened, her breath stuttered.

"Yes."

"You're willing to risk the weirdness that could follow when we end it?"

"That's the beauty of my plan. If we don't tell anybody about it, there won't be any weirdness."

"Except between us."

"I don't think so. We're older. Smarter. We've both been hurt. We know good sex isn't love and even if we did fall in love, we know love doesn't last. We also know what's important in life. Our kids. Neither one of us would do anything to hurt them. So we'd always be cordial when the family is together."

She bit her lower lip. She understood what he was saying because she'd considered a secret affair herself. But something hovered on the edges of her brain, a warning that was more of a feeling than a fact.

"So, what are your thoughts?"

She took a breath. Even as every nerve ending in her body tingled at the possibility, her brain held back.

"As much as I want to say yes, I need to think about it."

"Okay. You're working until Tuesday. By the

time you leave for Italy it will be Wednesday. Plenty of opportunity to think about it."

She hoped so because on Wednesday night they'd both be living in his villa, seeing each other every day—

It was no wonder he'd brought up the possibility of an affair. Spending that much time in the same space, their attraction would be off the charts.

Unless they controlled it. Or satisfied it. Giving in behind closed doors meant not fighting it twenty-four hours a day.

It also meant closeness and happiness with a guy who was charming and fun.

She swallowed. She hadn't wanted something the way she wanted this in years. "Okay. I'll think about it."

"Good. We'll talk when you get here."

She almost said goodbye to him, glad he wasn't going to belabor the issue, then she remembered the shoes. "Wait! I forgot to thank you for the shoes!"

He laughed. "Ah, yes. The shoes. I'm afraid I can't take credit. My assistant got them."

She frowned. "How did she know I needed them?"

"That I can take credit for. I phoned her on the way back to the villa that night to tell her what had happened and mentioned that I wanted you to have replacement shoes first thing in the morning. She volunteered to find them immediately so you could take them home with you."

"That was very kind of her. But they were at the hotel when I left for the airport. That couldn't have been more than four or five hours. She had to order them in the middle of the night."

"Probably."

"She lost sleep over my shoes?"

He laughed. "She loves her job and makes an extremely generous salary. She also likes to keep me happy. It wasn't a big deal."

He might not understand it, but it *was* a big deal. Still, she didn't say anything more about it, just said goodbye when they disconnected the call.

But at least now she knew what the negativity haunting her was all about. Telling her about the shoes, he'd sounded so much like Greg that their different stations in life stood out like neon signs.

Still—

Did it really matter that he had more money than some small countries, when they were only considering an affair? She'd wanted to marry Greg. She did not want to marry Lorenzo.

Just to have some fun.

She glanced around her silent living room. Because he was right. She wasn't entirely sure *he* was boring, but her life had definitely gotten quiet and predictable.

Still, her only daughter was about to marry his only son. One slip could ruin their wedding, and with them living in the same house the opportunities for slipups were too great. They would have no privacy. No space where it wasn't possible for someone to barge in on them. The very thing that made an affair seem like a necessity also made it an impossibility.

Her priority in Italy had to be wedding planning, not romancing the groom's dad.

Tired of thinking about it, she picked up the remote and turned on the news to distract herself. Monday morning, she and Pete attended the meeting with the doctor group and Tuesday she worked furiously, so she wouldn't have time to think about Lorenzo or the wedding or anything but the tasks she needed to accomplish. Then she caught a late-night flight on Tuesday night so she could sleep on the plane.

With the train ride, she arrived in Florence on Wednesday night. Her heart fluttered just thinking about seeing Lorenzo, who had said he was coming with the limo to pick her up, but being eager to see him was wrong. An affair might be fun, but if they were discovered it could ruin Riley's wedding.

She saw the limo just as her phone pinged with a text.

Something unexpected came up. Didn't come with the limo. I will see you when I get home. Lorenzo.

Her heart rate nosedived, but she scolded herself. She wasn't on board with a romance between them. So maybe not seeing him until they were in his house, around other people was a good thing?

Her phone pinged with another text. This one from Riley. She was in the limo only a few feet away. With things returning to normal with her daughter, thoughts about Lorenzo all but disappeared. She rolled her suitcase and duffle bag to the limo, smiling. Her daughter was getting married! Tomorrow, they would begin planning.

The driver opened the door. "Good evening, ma'am."

She smiled. "Good evening."

She slid inside and reached out to hug Riley. "It's so nice to see you!"

The driver closed the door.

Riley laughed. "It's nice to see you too."

"You didn't have to meet me. It's bad enough we're keeping the driver from going home and getting out of the cold."

Riley batted a hand. "He doesn't mind. He's paid extremely well."

Juliette glanced at her daughter. That was almost exactly what Lorenzo had said when they'd discussed her shoes and his assistant losing sleep to get them to her—the thing that reminded her of the huge gulf between her standard of living and the Salvaggios'.

She almost said something but decided against it. She didn't want to disturb this wonderful time with her daughter. Plus, the billionaire lifestyle was foreign to her. Maybe the Salvaggios really did pay their staff enough that they didn't mind doing personal favors in the middle of the night? She also knew nothing about the hours chauffeurs worked. This guy could be handling the night shift.

The nudge of discomfort wiggled through her again. She really didn't know anything about this world. She was a fish out of water. She didn't know about life on a vineyard, with a villa, and servants. She knew Manhattan. She knew doctors. She knew how to be the best at providing services for her clients.

She didn't know how billionaires lived. Having been so cruelly judged by Greg's dad at the funeral, she could be too sensitive about the Salvaggios' behavior. She needed to keep an open mind about Riley's prospective in-laws. Not make unfair comparisons.

After the driver tucked her suitcases in the trunk, they drove to the villa, chatting about the things Riley and GiGi had discussed before they'd put a moratorium on wedding planning, waiting for Juliette's arrival. Excited to hear everything, she forgot about the Salvaggios' station in life and even about feeling like a fish out of water. These two weeks would be all about her daughter.

Walking into the foyer, they removed their coats, which were taken by a man Juliette now assumed was the butler because he was there to take her coat every time she arrived. She'd simply accepted his presence the first two times she'd been to the villa. Today, realizing she'd be here for two weeks and needed at least a rudimentary understanding of how this household worked, she paid attention to what was going on.

Riley directed her to the sitting room. As they entered, GiGi rose. "We waited dinner for you."

Juliette walked to her, took her hands and kissed her cheek. "Thank you. I have to admit, I am starving. I slept on the plane, then wasn't hungry until I got off the train. I think it's the time difference."

GiGi and Antonio laughed. GiGi said, "Our

Riley had no trouble adjusting to the time difference."

Juliette didn't even take offense at GiGi claiming Riley as her own. GiGi was a wonderful woman who only wanted to make everyone happy. Even Lorenzo knew that.

She smiled. "Riley *is* younger, but if I remember correctly, she also had several trial runs last summer. What was it? One weekend in Italy. The next in Manhattan?"

Everybody laughed.

"They didn't see that they were falling in love," GiGi said. "But I did."

"You're a wise old woman," Lorenzo said from the bar.

His voice startled Juliette so much, she spun to face him. In his dark suit and white shirt, he looked his usual yummy self. She might have decided against a secret fling, but that didn't stop the warmth that shimmied through her or the way her breath bottomed out.

She told herself that was only because he was good-looking.

He motioned to the bar. "What can I get you to drink?"

"If everybody's having wine, wine is good with me."

His dark eyes held her gaze. "You know you're

allowed a before-dinner cocktail. Just because we make wine, doesn't mean we're purists."

She laughed. No one else did.

With a quick glance around the room, she realized GiGi, Antonio and Riley were so wrapped up in their own conversation they weren't noticing her and Lorenzo.

She said, "Wine is fine," but her voice came out deeper than it should, sexy, as if her hormones had taken over.

He smiled, poured her wine and brought it to her. As he handed it to her, he whispered, "You don't know how badly I want to kiss you right now. I missed the hell out of you."

Her stomach fell.

"Please, Juliette," he said, his voice back to normal volume. "Have a seat."

GiGi heard that and she gasped. "Where are our manners! I didn't mean to leave you standing there."

Juliette smiled. There was no way to tell an eighty-something woman that Juliette had been standing in the middle of the room mesmerized by her handsome son. And also no way she'd expected the kiss remark or her reaction to it.

All her good intentions about not having an affair wavered.

Still, she was a strong New York businesswoman. She could handle this.

She primly took a seat in one of the chairs flanking the sofa where Antonio, Riley and GiGi sat. Lorenzo took the chair across from hers, so they were looking at each other.

"I'm sorry I couldn't come with the limo to pick you up. Today was a day from hell for me. I barely got home in time to shower and change for dinner."

"Oh." He didn't have to explain himself to her, but it was considerate that he had.

He smiled and her heartbeat stuttered.

Seriously. The guy was gorgeous and suave and so sexy her nerve endings perked up every time he was around. Just as he said that it was a shame they'd never get to kiss, it suddenly also seemed a shame not to explore what was between them.

Couldn't they just sleep together once?

She was about to say no, that she didn't want to do anything that might make a mess of the wedding. But her romantic side cut her off, telling her an entirely different version of what might happen. One time of sleeping together couldn't mess up the wedding. Soon everybody would be so busy with the planning that they wouldn't notice anything but dresses and dishes and floral arrangements. They probably wouldn't even notice if she and Lorenzo behaved differently.

Though she didn't think they would. They

weren't giddy teenagers, or twenty-year-olds or even rambunctious thirty-year-olds. They knew how to act—

"Mom?"

Her head snapped up. "I'm sorry. Did you say something?"

"We were all wondering about your flight."

Across the coffee table, Lorenzo smiled knowingly at her.

"It was fine." She cleared her throat. "I had my laptop. After I slept, I did some work."

Antonio said, "Riley tells us you barely ever take a break."

"Running a small business is a lot different than running a conglomerate." Her wits restored, she immersed herself fully in the conversation. "I keep an eye on everything."

Lorenzo said, "We keep an eye on everything too."

"But it's so much more," Riley said, her voice dripping with awe. "You should see the things these guys manage, Mom."

The sense that she was out of the loop hit her again. She was accustomed to running something about the size of their winery. They managed that and God only knew what else. Obviously enough to impress Riley.

Lorenzo's phone buzzed. He glanced down at it, then rose. "Dinner is ready."

Antonio motioned for GiGi and Riley to walk before him. Lorenzo stealthily wound up beside Juliette. He whispered, "You look ravishing tonight. I love you in red."

Her body was covered in goose bumps. How could she not want to take advantage of this chemistry? Once. Just once.

"It's a sweater and jeans." She winced. "No time to dress for dinner."

He leaned closer. "I would have only imagined myself undressing you anyway."

His husky whisper tickled her ear. A shower of tingles fluttered through her. It appeared that if she really wanted this night, it could be hers. But it had to be on her terms.

CHAPTER SEVEN

WHEN THE CONVERSATION at dinner turned to the wedding, Lorenzo almost groaned. He did not want to get into that mess that could take hours and delay showing Juliette to her room.

Unfortunately, he knew Juliette was enjoying this. She'd realized she needed to participate fully in this wedding because this was the rest of her life. First, coming to Italy to help plan the wedding. Then coming to Italy for the wedding itself. Then visiting after the wedding to be part of the family her daughter was marrying into. She looked so calm about it that it appeared she was happy with her choice. If that was the case, that meant they could talk about gowns and bridesmaids and whatever else they had to choose tomorrow.

Tonight, she was his.

When they finished dessert in the sitting room, Antonio and Riley left through the back entry to go to their suite, taking GiGi with them so they could help her to the elevator, and he motioned for Juliette to precede him into the foyer. Just as he'd instructed the staff, her suitcase and duffle awaited them.

"What's this?"

"I wanted to be the one to show you to your room."

Her face scrunched as if she had no idea how to take that and he motioned her to the second elevator. He walked in behind her, carrying her duffel and rolling her suitcase. The door closed.

As the little car began to climb, she faced him. "I've been thinking about what you suggested in our phone conversation."

He almost smirked, hoping she'd spent all her time in Manhattan dreaming about him, but he realized that nothing with her was guaranteed. She could have been nearly seduced in their phone call and changed her mind on the flight over.

"And?"

"And I have an amendment to your suggestion."

He laughed. "Really? Formal negotiations?"

She sniffed. "We're too smart not to lay out our expectations."

"True. What are you thinking?"

"One night."

He turned to gape at her. "What?"

"One night."

"And we'll see how it goes?"

She laughed. "No. One night. You're too sexy to resist completely. But a woman's gotta know her limits."

He chuckled. "You think I'll be too much for you?"

"No. Our situation is too delicate. I don't want to ruin the wedding if our relationship is a bust." She peeked over at him. "You have to agree with that."

"I don't. We'll be keeping this a secret, remember? No matter what happens between us, the wedding won't be ruined because no one will know. Plus, you live in Manhattan. I live here. Anything we start could be over every time one of us gets on a plane and returns home."

She frowned, thinking about that. "Every time we're together would be like a one-night stand?"

"I suppose."

Her frown became a smile.

For some reason or another that smile grated on his nerves. "You like the idea of not being attached to me?"

"I have my reasons." She laughed. "You're the one who suggested we keep everything a secret. I could be insulted by that, but I'm not."

"That's the best way this works."

"I thought you said no attachments, just fun was how this worked."

"They mesh together. Put secrecy with no attachments and any margin for error has been taken care of."

She considered that, her frown returning, then as if she'd run through all the options and decided his reasoning was sound, she laughed. "I think you're right."

"I *am* right. These next few weeks have to be about Riley and Antonio. But that doesn't mean we can't enjoy some private time."

"Agreed."

The elevator door opened. He directed her to step out into the hall. "No more reservations about the wedding now?"

"It all hit me last weekend. Coming to Italy, becoming part of your family, is the rest of my life." She caught his gaze. "It's also why we have to be smart about us."

"Exactly."

He motioned for her to walk to the right. "There are three guest suites on this floor. I would let you have your pick, but I think you should take the first one."

She frowned.

He pointed to the end of the hall. "That door leads to my suite." He pointed at the door closest to it. "If I put you right beside me... Well, maybe no one would notice, but putting you here—away from my room—prevents anyone from questioning."

She rose to her tiptoes and kissed him. "You overthink."

He caught her elbows, keeping her close to him. "After the discussion we just had setting terms for something that happens naturally for most people, you have no room to talk."

"Are you really concerned that someone's going to question that we're on the same floor?"

"When Riley came to live with us, we moved Lorenzo down to the second-floor suite, which has a kitchen and sitting room to give them the option of eating alone or watching television alone sometimes. All the rooms up here are empty now. People should consider it the logical move."

She tilted her head. "There isn't a free room on the second floor?"

"Of course, there is."

"No one will wonder why I'm not by my daughter?"

He sighed. "Now who's overthinking?"

He opened the door onto a suite decorated in blues and pale greens and filled with flowers. Vases of bouquets sat on every flat surface. Tall vases. Short vases. Roses. Carnations. Lilies. Mums.

She faced him. "Pretty sure of yourself."

He caught her by the waist and hauled her to him, kissing her the way she deserved to be kissed. Thoroughly and without reserve. No one would see. No one could comment or care.

This was the moment he'd waited for.

She slid her arms around his neck. This time when he pulled her close, he felt her softness— through clothes. Not at all what he wanted. Without any hesitation, he reached for the hem of her sweater, as he kicked the door closed.

"Seems a shame to get rid of this. You look so good in it. But right now, I want to feel your skin."

The flutter of his fingers against her belly sent wave after wave of arousal through Juliette. She had never been so hot for someone. Probably because of the element of forbidden fruit, but she didn't care.

Knowing she had to distract herself or she'd melt into a puddle of need, she unbuttoned his jacket and let it fall to the floor. His tie followed suit and so did his silky white shirt, as he undid her jeans and she stepped out of them.

Standing before him in a red bra and panties, she admired his flat stomach, his chest, his muscular arms. But not for long. With a growl, he pulled her to him. Their bodies met and her heart shimmied, as their mouths merged in blissful union, tongues twining.

He reached around and unsnapped her bra. She reached down and unbuckled his belt. More clothes drifted away. His hand slid under her panties and along her bottom. She groaned with pleasure.

Without missing a beat in his kiss, he eased them to the bed. The feeling of being stretched out together almost overwhelmed her. But he didn't give her time to think. All she could do was feel. The roughness of his skin beneath her palm. The way his hand glided along her smooth thighs. With all thought gone and only feelings guiding her, she touched and tasted to her heart's delight. When they joined, she was so ready the heat of it was like an explosion. And when they reached the summit and tumbled over, her breath caught then drifted out on a moan of pure pleasure.

After a few seconds for each to recover, Lorenzo rolled away and flopped down on the pillow beside hers. "Only once you said?"

Her breaths came in ragged puffs. "Yeah, I said that, but your way is better."

He snorted. "We're gonna be sneaking away from the family to meet up for this every chance we can get."

She laughed.

He rolled over and pinned her to the bed. "Now, can we stop analyzing and let things happen naturally?"

She grinned at him. "I seem to remember you like things that happen naturally."

"Yes. I do."

He kissed her before she could say anything else. The kiss went on and on, warming her blood and her heart. Her blood could catch fire and she wouldn't care. It was the heart that worried her. She did not want her heart engaging. She wanted to maintain the distance she kept in all her relationships. No need for her heart to get involved. Given that she continually noticed ways they were different, and the horrible feeling of not belonging that filled her every time she did, she knew there was no way this could ever be permanent.

But as long as they were just having fun, seeing every goodbye as a potential end of anything between them, she didn't have anything to worry about.

Two hours later, Lorenzo woke up and looked at the clock. Skimming his hand down his face, he took a long, slow breath. Juliette roused.

He rose from the bed. "Sorry. Go back to sleep."

She eased into a sitting position. "Are you going to your room?"

He stepped into his trousers. "Yes. I get phone calls at all hours of the day and night. I don't want to disturb you."

As he slid into his shirt, she smiled. "Back to overthinking again?"

He bent down and kissed her. "No. The truth is I don't really overthink. I figure out ways to make things work." Socks in his jacket pocket, he stepped into his shoes. "Like this," he said motioning between them. "Just try to stop me from making love to you again."

Rather than argue, she busied herself straightening the bed sheet. "Well, if you insist."

"I'm going to do more than insist. After your two wedding planning weeks are up, we should fly to Paris."

She gasped. "That's the kind of thing that could get us caught."

He shrugged. "I don't see how."

"I've never been to Paris. I'll talk about it. I'll slip up."

"Then maybe we save Paris for after the wedding." He sat beside her on the bed. "I want to show you the city."

She smiled. "Okay. After the wedding."

She said it through her smile, but Lorenzo sensed hesitation. "You don't think we'll last that long?"

"You're the one who said every goodbye might be permanent. I'm just keeping it real."

He headed for the door. "Okay. You keep it real, and I will be the dreamer."

"It's all about balance."

He laughed. "I suppose it is."

He walked out of her room and headed down the hall to his suite.

No one had seen. No one had heard.

And he had no fear that Juliette would slip up. She was too concerned about her daughter not to monitor her every word.

That unexpectedly gave him pause. She really did overthink everything. He wasn't worried she'd zap the fun out of their relationship. Her overthinking sometimes made him laugh. Maybe it was male pride, but he wanted her to be as out of control with him as he was with her.

But she'd held something back as if she was afraid—

She was only afraid of hurting her daughter, messing up the wedding somehow, and he would see to it that they wouldn't.

He opened his suite door. Once she got comfortable with the idea that they wouldn't get caught, she would come around.

CHAPTER EIGHT

JULIETTE WOKE TO an empty bed the next morning. She yawned and stretched feeling wonderful, then a sense of foreboding shimmied through her. The man was a billionaire. Technically, she was a commoner, the way she'd been with Greg—

She ignored her thoughts. She and Lorenzo were having an affair. Nothing about their relationship was serious and certainly not permanent. If she was thinking of marrying the man, she might be panicking right now. But she wasn't. It didn't matter that how he lived was different than how she lived. All that mattered was that Lorenzo was sweet, handsome, sexy and so romantic she could still swoon from things that happened hours before.

She took in all the flowers in her room and laughed. He was such a charmer. Actually, he was such a charmer that he might have overlooked the fact that whoever helped him with this would tell the rest of the staff—

No. As head of the household, he'd probably sworn that person to secrecy. He was too certain they wouldn't get caught to ask someone to help him and not make sure they wouldn't spill the beans. He was also a very responsible guy. He'd told her about raising Antonio, about watching out for GiGi. He took his responsibilities seriously.

However he'd gotten these flowers in here, he'd been careful.

Which was one of the things she liked about him. He was a smart guy.

She glanced at the clock and sat up with a smile. It was only a little after seven. She was getting better about adjusting to the time difference. Which, technically, was her first hurdle. And she'd aced it.

She reached for her phone and saw that Riley had texted her.

In all the confusion last night, I don't think anyone told you breakfast is at eight in the dining room where we ate dinner last night.

She threw off the covers. Not only was she awake before noon, but she had time to dress for breakfast. Things were going her way.

Dressed in jeans and a peach sweater, she took the elevator to the first floor and easily found the dining room.

Walking in, she said, "Good morning, everyone."

Gentlemen, Lorenzo and Antonio rose. Both wore suits because they would soon be leaving for work, but Riley and GiGi were dressed comfortably.

Second hurdle down. Not only had she awoken on time, but also she'd dressed appropriately.

Then she caught Lorenzo's gaze and her stomach fluttered. He always looked yummy in a suit and tie, but today his eyes had a special sparkle.

The urge to smile at him almost overtook her. Instead, she pulled her gaze away and headed for the empty seat…right beside him.

No need to panic about his nearness. She could handle it.

"Thanks for the text, Riley. I had just awoken."

As she reached the chair, Lorenzo rose to pull it out for her. His hand grazed her forearm as she sat. Memories of their night before flooded her, but she ignored them.

GiGi said, "Breakfast is always at eight, though you don't have to be here if you want to sleep in. The kitchen staff will be happy to accommodate you."

All thoughts of Lorenzo fled. Making staff work to accommodate her didn't sit right, but something tapped the toe of her shoe. Her gaze nearly flew to Lorenzo, but she stopped it. She should have guessed he was the kind of guy who would play footsie.

"I like to get up early…" She cleared her throat when her voice came out scratchy. "Breakfast at eight will suit me."

Antonio gave her a confused look, but GiGi kept on talking. "Lunch is whenever we decide. Dinner is typically based on when these two—" she pointed at Antonio and Lorenzo "—get home from the office."

"There's fruit in the kitchen," Riley added. "Snacks. Crackers."

"And cookies," GiGi said with a laugh. "In case you need a little something to get you to dinner. Please help yourself."

The guy who usually took her coat walked in pushing a cart with plates of French toast, eggs, bacon and regular toast.

"This is Gerard, our butler," Lorenzo said. "Gerard, this is Juliette, Riley's mother."

He actually bowed. "Pleasure to meet you, ma'am."

Juliette froze. She had no idea if she should stand and shake his hand. A person always rose from their seat and shook the hand of a new business acquaintance, but this man was the butler.

Too much time went by for her to rise. She smiled and said, "It's a pleasure to meet you too."

He nodded before setting dishes on the table in front of Lorenzo, serving breakfast family style. Lorenzo handed a dish to Antonio and one to her, as Gerard left the room.

Luckily, her plate contained scrambled eggs, something she loved so she could occupy herself with that and forget about the uncomfortable situation. She took two spoonsful and passed them to GiGi.

In short order, all the plates made their way around the table. Juliette had taken only eggs, bacon and a piece of toast.

Lorenzo pointed at her food. "That wouldn't keep me until ten."

She cautiously caught his gaze. "I'm a light eater."

He smiled at her. Her breath stalled.

Riley said, "She always eats like a bird. It's how she stays so small."

"Not like this one," Antonio said, pointing at Riley, "who likes doughnuts."

Riley laughed. GiGi laughed. If Juliette had made a faux pas in how she'd reacted when being introduced to Gerard, no one had noticed…or cared. They didn't seem to be real sticklers for protocol, so maybe she could relax?

Or maybe she needed to do some research. Before they got down to wedding planning this morning, she would go online and research household etiquette when there were cooks, housekeepers and butlers. She knew all the normal things a person needed to know when dealing with business associates—including eating out at fancy restaurants—but she'd never personally interacted with a butler before—or lived in a house filled with servants. She would think this through and research accordingly.

They finished breakfast and Lorenzo and Antonio rose. Antonio bent down and kissed Riley who gave him the most wonderful smile.

Lorenzo caught her gaze as if telling her he wished he could kiss her, and she yanked her eyes away and got up from the table too. "I have a few things to do in my room, then I'll be down to start the wedding planning."

GiGi rubbed her hands together with glee. "I can't wait."

She left the dining room. Rather than take the elevator, she ran up two flights of stairs, the exercise helping her to release the odd mix of feelings she'd had at the dining room table. Her potential faux pas. Being so close to Lorenzo that she could smell his aftershave. The fight to keep her reactions normal around him—

And there he stood at the top of the stairs.

As soon as she'd taken the last step, he scooped her up into his arms, kissing her deeply. "Good morning."

She wanted to scold him. She should have scolded him for the flirty smile and the footsie. Instead, she blinked. "Good morning."

"I hated having to leave last night."

"If we want to keep this a secret, we need to take appropriate measures. And speaking of that—how did you get those flowers into my room without anyone seeing?"

"Everyone saw."

She gasped.

"Relax. I told Gerard that you wanted all the flowers so you could see your options for bouquets and centerpieces."

She stared at him.

He snickered. "As a cover story I thought it was pretty damned good." He kissed her again. "You are such a stickler for propriety."

She stepped back and crossed her arms on her chest. "Because I don't want to risk ruining the wedding."

"And I am careful."

"Playing footsie when everyone is in the room is not careful."

He sighed. "Fine. You are right. I will behave."

She shook her head with a laugh. "You're such a charmer that I think you're having a little trouble holding that back."

"Or maybe you bring out the charmer in me."

Her heart melted. He had a way of making her

feel special, but not like a princess, more like an equal. Which was probably why he was getting to her. She wasn't a princess, so she could shrug that off. But she was an equal. Maybe not in money. But she worked as hard as he did. She'd made the best out of her life the way he did.

That's why it was so easy to forget his life was different. In a lot of ways, they were alike.

He left for work, and she headed for her laptop to investigate etiquette with maids and butlers, chauffeurs, even the maintenance people. Twenty minutes later, proud of herself for getting on top of this, she left her room and walked into the sitting room. Riley sat alone, leafing through a book of floral arrangements.

Thinking of Lorenzo, she held back a laugh, and lowered herself to the sofa beside her. "Have you made any choices?"

Riley laughed. "A lot of choices. No final decisions. Though I understand you asked for some samples."

"Yes. I didn't so much want to see bouquets," she said, expanding on Lorenzo's story. "As I wanted to look at different kinds of flowers. Remind myself of what's out there."

Riley nodded, then she frowned. "It's a bigger job to pick something for yourself than it is for other people. Most of my clients are pleasantly surprised by what I choose. But I've got a hundred options they didn't even know were available."

"Don't stress!" She squeezed Riley's hand. "Let's just have fun."

"Agreed." She bit her lower lip, then drew in a long breath. "There's something else I'd like to talk about before GiGi gets here. I know you weren't happy with our engagement, and I just want to make sure you really are okay with everything."

Juliette smiled and squeezed Riley's hand again. "I'll admit I was a little taken aback when you first got engaged. But now, I'm getting caught up in things. The wedding. Your future children." She laughed. "*My* grandchildren. And all the lovely holidays we'll have together."

Riley blinked. "You really don't mind coming here for holidays?"

"It would be ridiculous for you and Antonio to drag your kids to Manhattan, when I can more easily get on a flight and come here." She glanced around at the beautifully appointed sitting room. "Being here is not exactly a hardship."

Wide-eyed, Riley said, "Wow. You totally changed your mind?"

"Totally."

Riley laughed "I've never seen you do that."

"I'm not unreasonable. When I'm wrong, I never stubbornly dig in my heels."

The perfect example was her relationship with Lorenzo. She'd thought one night…he disagreed. Now, she agreed with him. What they started could go on for a while. As long as he really could keep his feelings under control when they were in public.

She wished she could tell Riley that. They always discussed their relationships. But Riley had held back a bit about Antonio. Of course, their relationship began as pretending to be engaged in the hopes of lifting GiGi's spirits enough that she'd start her chemo. Juliette was keeping Lorenzo a secret because they'd made a deal knowing secrecy was the only way this worked—and she agreed with him.

She smiled at Riley. "You really love this guy?"

Riley rolled her eyes. "Remember the three I lived with?"

Juliette grimaced.

"Well, what I feel for Antonio is totally different. It's complete. It's overwhelming sometimes. He's thoughtful and kind. A hard worker who takes his responsibilities seriously…yet he's still romantic."

Juliette understood that perfectly. Still, this was her chance to make sure Riley did. "You don't think it's just infatuation? The guy *is* gorgeous and charming—"

Like his dad. With a room full of flowers, replacement shoes, compliments and suggestions that made her toes curl—Lord, no wonder Riley fell like a ton of bricks.

"And charming, gorgeous guys are very easy to fall for."

Riley shook her head. "No. This is real. We've talked about everything. Kids. Where we should raise them. Where we should live. What we want out of life." She sighed. "He's felt empty for a long time. So have I."

Her heart tweaked. She'd already realized that sometimes her life seemed hollow too. Lots of work. No deep emotion. Breakfast while she raced to her office. Takeout dinners alone. She understood what Riley was saying. Sometimes she wanted more. Then she would remember Greg dying and his dad telling her she was an upstart and remember that "more" frequently came with heartache and trouble.

"You and Antonio want the same things?"

"We want to be happy. But we also want to be fulfilled. You know the Salvaggios are committed to their land, their legacy."

Juliette nodded. "Lorenzo has mentioned it a time or two."

Riley perked up. "Antonio said you two were getting friendly."

Given what they'd done the night before, they were a lot more than friendly. "Yes. I like him. I like his sense of responsibility. If Antonio has that same sense, he's a good a guy."

"He really is, Mom. And we make each other happy."

Trying to be subtle, she said, "You realize you've changed the entire trajectory of your life for a man."

"No, I changed the entire trajectory of my life for love. For a purpose. For a future. Besides, I'm not abandoning my business. I'm expanding it. Someday, I'll be offering proposals all over the globe."

Juliette laughed. "I hope."

"I *know*. And not just because I'm strong. Because Antonio and I are a team."

"That's good."

"It *is* good. I finally don't feel alone."

Remembering the difficult years after Greg died, with his family disowning them and no other family to speak of, Juliette caught her daughter's hand. "You were never alone. You always had me."

"I know." She sighed. "But this is another level. I wish you could find this."

Juliette groaned. "Are you kidding? I'm too set

in my ways. Plus, I like being the boss. I don't think I'd do compromise as well as you do."

Riley laughed.

But Juliette suddenly saw that this was why neither she nor Lorenzo wanted a future. They'd both been burned, but more than that they'd both been alone too long to think they could suddenly become part of a couple.

Disappointment tightened her chest. She ignored it. Riley and Antonio wanted a future. They had space in their lives to compromise. They had space in their lives to grow. Lorenzo had duty and responsibilities. She had a company to run and a home in one of the most beautiful cities in the world. It had taken her decades to get here. To be satisfied. To be the boss. To have everything she wanted. What Riley and Antonio sought wasn't right for her anymore. And she didn't want to risk being hurt…or getting into a relationship that was wrong for her. In Manhattan, she was at the top of her game. Here, she'd had to research how to deal with a butler. She liked being at the top…being the one in control…better.

GiGi stepped into the room. "Great! We are all here. While you were upstairs, the designer arrived. I took him to the second-floor sitting room. He hung rough versions of all three dresses there. They're waiting for you to try them on."

Riley raced upstairs and GiGi led Juliette to the elevator that took them to the second floor. When they arrived in a big room that looked like another living room, Riley was in the adjoining room to the right. After a few minutes, she came out, wearing a simple white A-line dress, the designer, Pierre, following her.

As Juliette and Antonio's grandmother took seats on a sofa, GiGi said, "Do you like it?"

Riley smoothed her hand along the material. "This fabric for the real gown will be silk…" She paused. "But the fit is nice."

Juliette laughed. "If it's *nice*, it's not the one."

Riley returned to the adjoining room and came out in a second dress.

GiGi frowned. "Is it me or do both of the dresses look too plain?"

"I think the velvet cape is throwing you off, Riley," Juliette said. "Because it's so pretty you're letting it steal the show. But you won't have it on in the ballroom. You need a pretty gown. Let the cloak shine through the ceremony, but you're going to want something stunning for the reception. All three of these dresses are too simple."

GiGi nodded. "I agree."

"Do you have the book with your renderings?" Juliette asked Pierre.

"Of course." He went into the dressing room and returned with the book.

Juliette took it and flipped through Pierre's designs. When she saw the perfect dress, she said, "Ahh."

GiGi leaned in. "Ahh."

Riley raced over. She glanced down, then she laughed. "I think you're right."

GiGi smiled at Pierre. "Can you make a mock-up of this one for us?"

Lorenzo could tell something was up at dinner from the way Riley glowed, GiGi giggled and Juliette looked pleased. Not one of the three of them mentioned anything that should have caused so much excitement. They'd finalized a menu, made changes to the bouquets and flowers for the ballroom and put together a list of songs for dinner music to be played by the string quartet.

None of which should make his mother giggle.

Something was going on.

When it was time to retire for the night, no one even noticed that he and Juliette entered the elevator together. GiGi had long ago gone to bed and Antonio and Riley were headed to the sitting room of their quarters to watch a soccer match.

In the elevator, he waited a second before he

casually said, "So I take it the wedding planning went well today."

"We got a lot done. It's very convenient that we'll be having the wedding in the vineyard and the reception in your ballroom. No one to call to reserve space. No one to tell us no."

"There is a freedom to it."

"And GiGi showed me your outdoor space." She shook her head. "I wish they would wait until June so we could have the reception out there."

"That sounds like you haven't given up trying to persuade them to change the date."

She laughed. "Lord, no. That was just wishful thinking. They know what they want." She paused a second. "It might be because they're older than I was when I committed to Greg, but Riley and Antonio have talked about things that it never occurred to me to discuss with Greg. We were in love. We were pregnant. I felt the hand of fate. We simply moved in together and made a life. And Riley and I both saw how that turned out."

The elevator door opened. "Are you saying Antonio and Riley might have done everything right?"

She smiled. "Maybe."

He frowned. "Are you looking for guarantees?"

"Nope. I'm just experienced enough to know that no one does *everything* right."

His laugh filled the third-floor hall. He loved laughing with her. He loved having someone he didn't have to measure his words with. He loved hearing her perspective, even if it sometimes didn't match his.

It felt so good to be himself.

She opened the door to her suite, and he followed her inside, closing the door behind them.

When he gathered her into his arms and kissed her, she didn't argue or question. She simply melted. She had his clothes off before he managed to get hers off but once they were on the bed, he didn't care who was taking the lead. He just wanted to hold her and touch her and taste her until they were both so far gone, they forgot what day it was.

The only thing that marred the perfection of sleeping with her was not actually getting to sleep with her. He had to re-dress and go back to his suite. Before he reached it, he realized he was hungry and glanced at the stairway. By now, Riley and Antonio's game should be over, but it didn't matter. They were in their own room.

Not that he cared. This was his home. He could go to the kitchen for a snack. What could they say if he ran into them?

He ambled down the stairs and into the kitchen for some crackers. Deciding to take the entire box to his room, he left the kitchen and almost walked into Riley.

"Hey!" She glanced at his suit. "What have you been doing for the last two hours?"

He felt his face redden. *This* was what they could say! Normally, he would have changed out of his suit and into sweats or even pajamas and a robe once he went to his room. Yet here he was still in his suit. It was one of those mistakes he'd promised Juliette he wouldn't make.

"I was talking on the phone with a friend. He called right as I got to my room. I didn't get a chance to change."

Antonio popped out and joined Riley. "Oh! What friend?"

"Frank."

"You don't know anybody named Frank."

He snorted. "Antonio. You do not know everybody I know! Frank's from the States. He and his wife are in Florence on vacation."

Riley said, "Oh! That's nice."

Antonio smiled approvingly. "You should invite them here to see the vineyard."

He gaped at his son. Being in love was making Antonio incredibly kind and generous.

Unfortunately, Frank wasn't real.

Thinking quickly on his feet, Lorenzo said, "They're going home tomorrow. Which was why he called tonight—to say goodbye." He displayed his crackers. "And I'm saying good night to you."

As if not hearing him, Riley frowned. "If you spent two hours on the phone with him, you could have gone into town and had a drink together," she said. "And taken my mother. She could use some fun."

Lorenzo knew for a fact she'd had plenty of fun that night.

Antonio said, "You know, Marco will be at the wedding."

Lorenzo worked to hide a scowl. He did not like the idea that Antonio planned to fix up Juliette and Marco. Still, he avoided the topic by saying, "I should hope he'll be at the wedding. He's your godfather." He headed up the stairs. "But right now, I'm going to bed. Good night."

On the second floor, he turned to the left to climb the rest of the stairs to the third floor and his suite. At the top, he pulled out his phone. As he walked down the hall, he texted Juliette.

Ran into the kids in the hallway. Told them I was on the phone with a friend all night. You don't really need to know that because you were in your room and wouldn't know that I'd talked to a friend—

He sighed and deleted the text. She really didn't

need to know that. Getting accustomed to keeping this a secret really was going to be harder than he'd first thought.

He loosened his tie, then opened the door of his five-room suite that was more of an apartment. Loneliness hit him in a wave, but he knew why. He wasn't so much lonely as he was hungry for Juliette's company.

He wanted to sleep with her. In his big bed.

That probably made him a chauvinist…at the very least politically incorrect. But he was too tired to care.

In the morning, he would probably kick himself for letting those emotions seep in. He told himself it was just exhaustion, took off his clothes and fell face-first on the soft comforter.

When he awoke late, he didn't panic. He simply showered and went downstairs to breakfast. Antonio and Riley were finished eating and getting ready to start their day. GiGi dawdled over coffee.

He wanted to ask where Juliette was. Instead, he said, "What's on the agenda for the day, GiGi?"

"More wedding planning. Juliette will be down in a minute. She slept in."

He hid a smirk. He was not the only one who'd been tired out the night before. "She slept in?"

"Yes. She texted a few minutes ago, said she'd shower and be right down."

He almost laughed. He thought it was cute that she had trouble adjusting to the time difference and even cuter that they tired each other out so thoroughly that they'd both slept in.

He told himself to stop having thoughts like that. Dreamy, sexy things were good…but thinking them cute? That had too much of a feeling of connection to it. Still, he might not want forever with her, but he did like her. He liked her a lot.

And he intended for them to completely enjoy what they had, while it lasted.

CHAPTER NINE

THE DAY BEFORE Juliette's two-week visit was over, Antonio and Lorenzo were in his office in Florence immersed in creating a five-year plan for a new project when his phone buzzed.

They glanced at each other.

"Didn't you tell your assistant to hold all calls?"

Lorenzo sighed. "I did." He hit the button to answer. "Yes?"

"I'm sorry, Mr. Salvaggio," his assistant said, her voice coming through the phone's speaker. "But Annabelle Lindstrom is here to see you."

At the mention of his ex-wife's name, Lorenzo held back a groan. But, remembering she was Antonio's mother, he simply handed the visit off to his son. "Go talk to your mom."

"I'm sorry." His assistant's voice came out of the speaker again. "But she's here to see both of you. She was very clear about that. Do you want me to take her to the conference room?"

Antonio glanced at Lorenzo, obviously gauging his father's mood before he said, "Yes. Ask her if she'd like coffee. Because we might need a minute before we get to her."

Lorenzo rose. "We don't need time. Take her back to the conference room and Antonio and I will be right there."

As Lorenzo disconnected the call, Antonio said, "Are you sure?"

He snorted. "Antonio, your mother might be a thorn in my side, but she's your mother. We always treat her with respect."

Antonio said, "We do."

"Okay, then. Let's go."

They walked to the conference room and entered through a side door. Annabelle was already there, staring out the window at the streets of Florence. Her shiny dark hair gleamed in the sunlight pouring in, despite the cold morning.

She turned as they entered. "Antonio!" She raced over to hug her son.

Antonio returned her hug.

Lorenzo studied her, not quite able to put his finger on what was different. She pulled away from Antonio and faced Lorenzo.

"It's nice to see you too, Enzo."

He snorted. It really had been a while since he'd seen her. No one except GiGi called him Enzo anymore. Hearing her say it sent waves of memories through him. None of them good.

Still, he said, "It's nice to see you, Anna."

"You're probably wondering why I'm here…"

Lorenzo wasn't. She undoubtedly needed money—

Except she usually called him for that. They hadn't had a visit in forever.

She faced Antonio with a smile. "I heard you got engaged."

Antonio grinned. *"Sì."*

"Is your fiancée here?"

"She doesn't work here. She has her own company."

"In Florence?"

Antonio motioned for his mother to sit on the couch of the sitting area in the corner of the big room, then sat beside her. "Yes, she is moving her corporate offices here." He laughed. "Her name is Riley. She's American."

"American!"

"Sì. She's beautiful and kind and everything I've ever wanted."

Anna took her son's hands. "That's wonderful."

"The wedding's in January," Lorenzo said carefully.

She gasped. "So soon?"

"Yes. We are happy. We want to have children. We want to start our life together now. No waiting."

She smiled prettily—

And Lorenzo realized what was different. She was sober.

Weird sensations cascaded through him. He had no idea what to say. What to ask. Why she wanted to see them. Except that she probably wanted an invitation to the wedding. She *had* known Antonio had gotten engaged. She hadn't come to congratulate him. She'd come to insinuate herself into his life again.

Antonio said, "The wedding's here at the villa. So is the reception."

She squeezed their son's hands. "It's cold in January for an outdoor wedding."

Antonio laughed. "We know. We don't care. Your invitation will have the details."

She clutched her chest as if surprised. "I'm invited?"

Antonio said, "Of course!"

"I don't know what to say."

Lorenzo leaned against the windowsill. "Antonio, why don't you see what's taking my assistant so long with that coffee?"

He gave Lorenzo a confused look, but nodded and left the office.

Annabelle caught his gaze. "You're not happy I'm here."

A statement not a question.

"Annabelle, Antonio has never been so on

track. His fiancée is the sweetest woman I've ever met. They know what they want. And they are full of prewedding joy. Do not screw this up for them."

Her chin rose. "I'm sober now."

Foreboding sent warning after warning through him. Annabelle might not have made an actual demand for anything and might have stayed congenial, but she'd gotten what she wanted: an invitation to the wedding. He vividly remembered this kind of behavior from her. It was usually the calm before the storm. Play nice until she was back in his good graces, then push for something else. Whatever that was this time, she would be sneaky about getting it. Maybe even approach Antonio privately.

His blood heated with anger. Still, he remained calm. "I'm glad you're sober. But it doesn't change the fact that you will do irreparable damage to your relationship with your son if you ruin his wedding."

Annabelle happily said, "I won't."

How many times had he heard that?

Antonio arrived with the tray of coffee. "Since I was headed this way, I decided to save Maria a trip."

Having said his piece, Lorenzo headed for the door. He didn't have to be here for the rest of the mother and son time together. "I have a lunch appointment." Not true. Just an excuse to leave without offending her. "But you two enjoy your visit."

Annabelle protested. "No! Stay! I want to hear how you are too."

"I'm fine," Lorenzo said easily, casually, and even managed a smile. "You two are the ones who need to catch up."

Outside the conference room door, he ran his hands down his face. He hoped her sobriety lasted forever. He hoped, for Antonio's sake, she was ready for a real relationship. But he knew the drill. This visit was only the beginning. He would not let his guard down for thirty seconds around her, and he would watch her like a hawk at the wedding.

As he returned to his office, he considered calling Juliette, if only to talk this out. He even pulled his phone from his pocket—

But he paused.

Their little fling was exactly that. A fling. He would not in any way, shape or form burden her with the vagaries of his life or share his troubles.

If he called, it would be to hear her pretty voice or laugh about something. There would be nothing serious between them.

Ever.

For both of their sanities.

So maybe the reason he reached for his phone

was because he just wanted a chance to hear her laugh? To think about the fun, happy things he always thought about when he was with her.

For that, he wouldn't call her. He would take her to lunch so his excuse to Annabelle wouldn't really be a lie.

Maybe he should call GiGi and try to find her? Juliette had mentioned something about sightseeing that morning. But she hadn't said where. GiGi would know.

Juliette spent the first few hours of the morning playing gin with GiGi. When Lorenzo's mother tired out and went upstairs for a rest, she had the driver take her to town to look for a wedding gift for Riley and Antonio, then have lunch somewhere interesting.

But riding in the limo to go shopping, she'd felt ridiculous. She was a capable driver who should have simply used one of the cars in the big garage. It was weird to be driven to shop for a few hours. Especially since she might be part of the Salvaggios' extended family, but she wasn't actually one of them.

She refused to forget that.

She walked along Via Tornabuoni, looking at the offerings in the artisan boutiques, but nothing felt like a wedding gift. Realizing she'd probably end up buying a gift for the kids online, she shifted gears and became a sightseer, enjoying the way the city could be quaint in some places and sophisticated in others. The sights and sounds—and the scents of food and freshly baked bread and treats—all gave her a sense of being somewhere unique, somewhere wonderful.

She pulled up the collar on her coat. The first of December air was freezing, making her think about how cold an outdoor wedding would be in the middle of January.

Her phone rang. The busy street almost drowned out the sound but she'd caught the phone before it stopped ringing, ducking under a canopy to answer it.

Seeing the caller was Pete, she winced. "What's wrong?"

"I know I promised I wouldn't call you, but something happened late yesterday that was weird."

Realizing it was six o'clock in the morning in Manhattan and he was already in this office, she knew this was serious. "Weird? What does weird mean?"

"Your ex's parents' doctor called to arrange for our services."

At first, she froze, then her business instincts kicked in. "Are you sure they are who you think they are?"

"I did the usual investigations that we do on

all potential clients, financial, criminal, and personal."

Those checks were run to determine what level of services the client could afford, and also to ensure they weren't sending an unsuspecting nurse into a bad situation.

"Not only do they have the same last name—Finnegan—but they had a son Greg who died."

Her stomach plummeted. "Okay. That still could be a coincidence."

"Juliette," Pete said sympathetically. "The timelines match up. Riley's age now and the age she was when her father died were my guidelines."

Her muscles froze. They probably were Greg's parents. She had to face that. Handle it. "Okay."

Pete continued. "Apparently Mrs. Finnegan is suffering from dementia. She's not that far gone, but her husband is ten years older than she is and can't care for her at all."

Juliette mumbled, "I never knew about their age difference." She basically knew very little about them. Greg rarely spoke of them. She'd always believed there was a rift of some sort between them. After he died, she realized she'd been the rift.

Pete very kindly said, "Should we say we're too busy to take the job?"

"No. We are in the business of taking care of

people. Call the doctor and say we'll be doing our usual intake visit before we commit and arrange a date with him for that. Normally, I would be the one to do it, but they probably need help now and I'm in Italy another day, then the day I get back to Manhattan I'll be jet lagged. You'll need to do it."

He said, "Okay, boss."

They disconnected the call, and Juliette glanced around the quaint street that had so enthralled her and tried to get back her happy feelings. She refused to let the past ruin her afternoon. Even if these were Greg's parents, too much time had gone by to harbor anger or bitterness. She would treat this couple like any other clients who needed the help of the nurses she employed. Nothing more. Nothing less. Simply people who needed help that she could give.

But a weird heaviness followed her as she walked out from under the canopy. Refusing to give into it, she ignored it, once again huddling into her coat to protect herself in the freezing December air. She thought of Riley's wedding again, trying to figure out what to wear so she didn't shiver through the ceremony. Even a long-sleeve gown wouldn't provide enough protection—

It didn't matter. A January wedding in a very

cold vineyard was what Riley and Antonio wanted. That's what they would have.

She wouldn't let herself make the connection of how she respected her child's wishes and how Greg's parents had walked all over his. Because she didn't know that for sure. It was one of the things that had haunted her after he died. He could have married her hundreds of times. She hadn't wanted a big wedding. Only him. But they'd never made it official, making it easy for his parents to kick her out because she'd been too stunned by his death to fight them.

She'd never even tried to get child support because she'd been so damned determined to make it on her own and part of her was glad. She was as successful as she was because of needing to prove she wasn't an upstart.

And she had.

On her way up the street, scouting for a restaurant, she saw a black limo, one that had the Salvaggio Vineyards logo on the rear bumper.

She took a few steps closer. The back window slowly lowered. Lorenzo said, "Hey, know any beautiful women who would like to have lunch?"

All her thoughts of the past disappeared. Her heart lifted. "I was just looking for a restaurant."

He opened the limo door and eased out. "Where would you like to eat?"

"I'm a stranger here. You choose." Remembering her jeans and sweater under her navy pea coat, she added, "And make it somewhere I'm dressed appropriately for."

He stopped in front of her and kissed her. "To me you're always beautiful."

She laughed. Dear God, the man could pull her out of any unwanted mood. "Seriously? Flirting on a public street?"

"I enjoy wooing you."

Yeah, she liked it too. But they *were* on a public street. She glanced around. The old stone buildings had a lot of windows. Anybody could be watching them. "Where are Riley and Antonio?"

"Riley's working from the villa and Antonio's at the office. We're fine."

Her phone rang. Worried it might be Pete again, she dug it out of her purse and glanced at the caller ID. Not recognizing the number, she considered it might be the Finnegans' doctor and gave Lorenzo the *hold on one second* signal as she answered.

"Hello?"

"Hello, sweet Juliette," GiGi said.

She laughed with relief. "Hello, GiGi. What's up?"

Lorenzo frowned at Juliette, as she said, "You know, it's funny you called. I've been shopping in town and the cold is brutal. That made me think about what I'd be wearing to the wedding ceremony. What do you suggest for a coat for me? I'm wearing a gown, so I'm half tempted to do something like a cloak too...the way Riley is." She listened while GiGi talked. "We could make it a theme."

His frown disappeared as she laughed again. He loved her laugh, but more than that, he loved how good she was to GiGi, treating her like a friend. His mother had lost a lot of her friends. Juliette was a good fit.

"Okay. So, we're all wearing cloaks and there's an engagement party this weekend."

His eyes widened. *Engagement party?*

She batted her hand, giving him the universal symbol to simmer down. There was nothing to get excited about.

Then she said, "Goodbye. I'll see you this afternoon sometime."

She disconnected the call and tossed her phone into her purse again.

He stared at her. "An engagement party?"

"Antonio and Riley just decided they wanted one, and Antonio called GiGi. She called me."

He shook his head and directed her to walk up the street. "I know why. Antonio's mother visited this morning."

She met his gaze. "Is that unusual?"

"Yes. They rarely see each other. And you know how he's been lately…the world's a beautiful place and people are wonderful."

She chuckled. "That's the love hormones."

"Exactly. Anyway, he invited her to the wedding."

She winced. "She *is* his mother."

"I know. And realistically I want her there but she's a problem. I'll probably spend most of the wedding keeping an eye on her."

She squeezed his forearm. "I know. It's what you do."

"I had hoped to dance with you." He caught her gaze. "If only once."

"We can dance at the engagement party."

"No. She'll be there too. That's why Antonio wants a party. I'm guessing he's giving her a trial run to make sure a big gathering isn't too much for her sobriety."

Juliette's eyes widened. "She's sober? That's great news!"

He took a breath. He hadn't wanted to burden her with all of this, but she would be at the engagement party and wedding. She had to know what to expect.

"If we are lucky, maybe this time it will work for her."

"Let's hope so."

Her reaction was so calm and kind that his

spirits lifted a bit. Not only was she good to his mother, but she wasn't the type of person to panic over potentially bad news. She thought of Antonio first. Which made it nice to talk to her about it. He was almost glad that GiGi had called. Having her to sort it out with, it all seemed smaller somehow.

They reached the restaurant and he motioned for her to enter before him.

She laughed. "A pizza place?"

"Real pizza," he said, then led her to a booth in the back. After giving the server their orders, he leaned across the table. "I'm sorry I had to tell you about Annabelle. I like our relationship to be about fun. But you need to be prepared."

"I'm fine. In fact, whatever you need, I'll help you."

"That's the other reason I'm glad I could tell you. I'll probably need someone to help me keep an eye on her." He took her hands. "Thank you."

She said, "You're welcome," then she grimaced. "I actually have something I wasn't going to tell you either."

He glanced at her. "Really?"

"Greg's parents' doctor called my agency. His mother needs a private nurse."

The server returned with their drinks, giving him a moment to absorb that news.

As she left, Juliette looked at a picture of the

pizza on the menu. "This isn't so different from ours. The crust's a little thicker."

"There's also no sauce. We use real tomatoes."

"Oh."

He wasn't sure if she was trying to distract him, but he hadn't forgotten what they were talking about when their drinks had arrived. "You were saying your ex's parents are about to become your clients?"

She set her glass down. "It's what my company does. We help people."

The thought of her being kind to the parents who had evicted her burned through him like hot coals. "They hurt you."

"They are old and sick now. My company's mission statement is that we provide good care and human kindness to people who need it. That mission would be meaningless if I turned someone away."

He leaned across the booth and kissed her. "You are a good soul."

"Yeah, and it might just come back to bite me in the butt."

Wanting to support her, the way she supported him about Annabelle, he thought that through and said, "Or you could get the opportunity to show them what they missed."

"I'm not a hundred percent sure it's them, but it would be a hell of a coincidence if it wasn't.

Still, they must not have recognized my name, or they would have shifted their doctor in another direction. If they don't remember me, there's no reason for me to tell them who I am. Pete's doing the intake interview. I'll let him figure out what they need and assign staff, then I'll trust my extremely talented nurses to do their job. I won't even have to see the Finnegans."

He smiled at her. She was probably the most levelheaded person he knew. "Look at us… I'm rooting for my ex to stay sober so she can have a relationship with my son and whatever grandchildren he gives us, and you're being the most generous woman in the world."

She shook her head. "Not hardly. Just adhering to my mission statement."

He could see from the determination in her eyes that she believed that, but he saw more. So much more. He saw enough that his heart stumbled. He didn't think he'd ever met anyone like her. She was certainly Annabelle's polar opposite. Antonio's mother always wanted the spotlight. Never helped anyone because she never thought about anyone but herself and having fun.

Warmth filled him. "You know…maybe we get our pizza to go?"

"And eat it at your house?"

"And eat it in the nice little hotel you stayed

at the first time you were here. We could spend the afternoon together."

She laughed. "Eating pizza in bed?"

He grinned. "This affair is about fun... We both just had a weird morning. We need some fun. Plus, you're leaving tomorrow. I don't want you to forget me."

She laughed. "As if I could."

They got their pizza in a to-go box and strolled up the street to the limo, which took them to her former hotel. When they registered, he asked for champagne to be brought up to their room. It arrived only a minute or two after they'd stepped inside.

He poured two glasses, and they sat on the bed and sipped indulgently.

"This is great."

"I told you affairs with me were fun."

She laughed. He took the glass from her hand and set it on the bedside table of the small room so he could kiss her. She had no idea what a wonderful person she was. How kind. Even having reservations about her daughter's wedding, she'd listened to Antonio and Riley, watched them and come around to their way of thinking. Now she'd be taking care of Riley's grandparents, who'd not only kicked her out of her condo; they'd never acknowledged Riley.

If he wanted to spend a few minutes enjoying

her company, thanking the heavens that she was in his life, he was not going to stop himself. She deserved to be pampered.

They could go back to having fun when she returned from Manhattan for the engagement party, but today he wanted to love her.

CHAPTER TEN

Two HOURS LATER, Juliette kissed Lorenzo and walked into the bathroom as if she were the happiest woman alive, but once the door closed behind her, she leaned against it with a sigh.

Making love after their difficult mornings had been wonderful. She'd never felt so close to anyone. Her heart had swelled with ridiculous emotion. She would call it love but they didn't know each other well enough to be in love. Even Antonio and Riley had known each other for a few months. She and Lorenzo had basically just met…

A little over two weeks ago.

It wasn't love.

She'd promised herself she would not let her heart get involved, but having someone to talk to about her life was a little too nice to ignore. Yes, she talked to Marietta and Pete, but they were employees and there was only so far a boss could go with her confidences to maintain enough distance that she could be a good employer. She didn't want to burden them with her troubles, but talking to Lorenzo didn't feel like burdening him. It felt like confiding in a trusted friend.

And she'd loved him confiding in her too. He trusted her. Not in the one-friend-trusting-another way. In that deep down, almost spiritual way that two people could when they really understood each other.

After washing her face, she walked out of the bathroom and swooped her jeans off the floor. "Are we going back to the villa separately or together?"

"Did you make arrangements for one of the drivers to pick you up?"

"Yes. In a half hour in front of Gucci."

He grabbed his watch from the bedside table and winced. "I'll get you there with my limo." He rolled out of bed. "Then I'll go back to work, telling Antonio I ran into a friend."

She laughed. "Let's see… So far, you've been continually running into friends and had a two-hour phone conversation with a guy you made up… What was his name? Frank?"

"I should have never told you that."

"I can say I was shopping all day. But you may need to come up with a better excuse."

He laughed. "I could say I ran into *you* and we had lunch and shopped together."

She grimaced. "Maybe next time."

"Why?" He walked over and slid his arms around her. "It's a reasonable excuse for why I didn't come back to work. Instead of shopping, we could say we got pizza and were talking about the wedding." He stopped and grinned devilishly. "Or I could say I was telling you about an investment that might interest you."

She bit her lower lip thinking, then said, "I do have investments."

"See! Now we can take the same limo home."

She shook her head. "You are a conniver."

"No. I am always thinking of ways to make things work."

She had to give him that. She canceled her ride, and they took his limo back to the vineyard. The foyer was empty when they walked inside, so they could share the elevator to the third floor without raising suspicions. She told herself to stop worrying because no one was paying attention to them. No one was even there to see them.

But the next morning, Juliette wasn't surprised that she needed to go to Florence for her flight at the same time that Lorenzo needed to go to work. Still eating breakfast, GiGi, Antonio and Riley said quick goodbyes, seemingly accepting the excuse that he would be dropping her off at the train station on his way to work.

Walking to the limo, she considered saying something about his casual way of doing things,

but just as her worries about arriving home together the day before had been for nothing, their
kids and his mom had taken it as no big deal that
they were riding into town together.

He walked her inside the terminal and stopped
in front of her and straightened her scarf. "Sleep
on the flight, if you can."

"That works coming to Italy, but I think it
might backfire on the way home."

He chuckled. "No. It pretty much works both
ways. But you're still going to have some jet lag."

"Yeah. I did the last time."

He glanced around then gave her a quick kiss
before he walked away. He turned to wave goodbye, then quickened his steps to walk back to
the limo.

She shook her head. He thought he was being
careful, but she always thought of cities as being
like small towns in some ways. You never knew
who your waitress or cab driver knew and anything you said or did in public could become
gossip. She rarely said anything significant in
a public place.

He thought a quick look around handled everything.

She arrived in New York a little before nine
o'clock. Though it was the middle of the night
in Italy, it really wasn't even bedtime in Manhattan. At her condo, she caught up on emails.

The third one from Pete made her frown.

Finnegan appointment pushed to Thursday morning.

If she wanted to, she could handle it.

Confusing thoughts bombarded her. She made herself a bourbon and told herself to forget it, let Pete do the intake as planned, but she couldn't. If nothing else, she was curious about the people who'd rather be alone than acknowledge their only grandchild.

With a sigh, she returned to her computer and emailed Pete that she'd be doing the intake visit with the Finnegans.

The time difference and her nerves conspired to keep her up all night, so at seven o'clock, she showered and dressed, then left her apartment to find a bagel before she headed for the Finnegans'.

When the elevator door opened on a big sitting room, she saw why the building's doorman had punched in a code rather than tell her their floor number. The elevator was the front door to their penthouse. She also saw that the area needed a good cleaning. Dust had accumulated on lamps and end tables. She swore there was a cobweb on the top valance of the drapes.

She winced. The place was also hopelessly out of date, as if it had been frozen in time—

Her heart stuttered. Maybe they'd stopped caring when Greg had died?

Doctor Art Jenkins walked into the sitting room, his hand extended to shake hers. "Thank you, Juliette. I appreciate this."

"I'm happy to be here."

"It's why everyone loves your company. It's more than a job to you."

She said simply, "Yes," as the feeling of having traveled back in time enveloped her.

He motioned for her to follow him from the formal sitting room into a family room. She could see the old-fashioned French Provincial dining room furniture against the backdrop of Manhattan displayed through a wall of windows. A sense of their loneliness and desolation filled her. She understood perfectly. For years, she had missed Greg too.

As they entered the family room, an old man rose. Greg's dad. She'd only seen him at the funeral, but she'd spoken to him afterward. She easily recognized him as an older version of the man who'd humiliated her.

"This is Walter Finnegan." He faced Walter. "Walter, this is Juliette Morgan."

She offered her hand to shake his. He took it

with a weary smile. "I'm sorry. I just can't care for her."

He looked barely able to care for himself.

Upstart. No social climber will benefit from my son's death.

She released his hand, let the memories drift away as her work personality easily kicked in. "Please, Mr. Finnegan. Your situation isn't unusual, and my staff is more than capable."

The doctor motioned for them to sit.

"If you don't mind my saying this, I think you could benefit from a little help too."

He snorted. "I wouldn't mind some assistance."

She smiled kindly, as she glanced down at the intake sheet. The man was ninety. He might have a cook and a negligent housekeeper, but those kinds of employees didn't do personal things like assist with dressing or showers. Plus, once her employees were on staff, they could add a little accountability for the housekeeper.

They talked for ten minutes, and then she was taken back to Greg's mom's bedroom. Rachel Finnegan sat on a chair by the window, toying with her long hair, staring out at the city.

Art Jenkins said, "Rachel?"

She turned with a smile. "Good morning, Doctor." She glanced at Juliette and frowned. "Do I know you?"

Juliette shook her head. People with dementia frequently asked questions like that. Not for one second did she think Greg's mother recognized her.

"No. I'm with a home nursing agency. We'll be coming in to help you from now on."

"Help me what?" she demanded. "Help me lose my jewelry? Help me spend my money?"

Walter faced Juliette. "I'm sorry. The dementia turned her into a totally different person."

"Don't be sorry," Juliette said. "This is part of her disease."

Greg's parents were old and helpless. Their cook might feed them, but they needed help with hygiene and maybe someone to read to them or play games with them to keep their mental acuity as high as possible. Juliette's staff could make their final years much more comfortable.

The doctor walked her to the elevator. "Your company can take them on?"

"Yes. We probably should have been called sooner." The elevator arrived and the doctor got on with her. "How long has she been like this?"

"Two years."

The doors closed and they started down to the lobby. "It looks like two years since she's had a haircut."

He shook his head. "Walter just kept being

positive, thinking she'd bounce back, and she would want to take care of it herself."

"We're glad to help. My staff will contact your office to set up the bulk of the arrangements, including a schedule. You will also need to give us authorization to look at their medical reports so we have the full picture." Though she knew the answer, she asked, "There are no other close relatives who could sign papers or make arrangements?"

"Just me."

"You're a relative?"

"Not a relative. I was their son's friend. I have power of attorney."

She took a quiet breath but didn't react. Yet another person Greg hadn't introduced her to.

"He died and because I was their doctor I sort of stepped in."

The elevator doors opened. "That was kind of you."

"No. That's life."

Didn't she know it.

The doctor stayed on the elevator, obviously to return to the Finnegan penthouse.

"You'll hear from my staff."

She left the building not quite sure what she was feeling. She hadn't hated Greg's parents her entire life. She hadn't let herself think of them.

If she felt anything it was sorrow that they

were so alone when they hadn't had to be. Riley could have filled the empty spaces in their lives, but they had preferred for them to remain empty.

Confused about her feelings for them, Juliette threw herself into work when she returned to her office. At the end of the day, she was seated at her desk with a full view up the hall to the reception area when the main door opened, and Lorenzo walked in. Wearing a black cashmere overcoat and black leather gloves, he looked every inch the sophisticated gentleman that he was—with a little bit of bad boy thrown in when his unruly hair shifted along his collar when he moved his head.

Her mouth lifted into a smile. Her whole body began to tingle—

Then she remembered that there could still be stragglers in the office and any one of them could call Riley and tell her anything that happened between her mother and soon-to-be father-in-law. Whatever his reason for being here she did not want anyone on the staff of her company *or Riley's* to hear it.

She rose and scooted around her desk, then changed her mind. It was close enough to seven o'clock that she could also leave for the day. She grabbed her coat and purse and raced up to the reception area as quickly as she could.

"Lorenzo!" she said, walking past the empty

receptionist desk. Sissy would have gone home at five o'clock.

Lorenzo faced her with a smile. "Juliette—"

"I was just on my way out," she said, catching his elbow and steering him toward the door again. When they were in the empty hall on their way to the elevator, away from any employees who might still be in the office, she said, "Why are you here? Did the kids break up? Oh my God, is there something wrong with Riley?"

He laughed. "Riley is fine. I just…" He cleared his throat. "My house is wedding central. Gifts are beginning to arrive."

The elevator came and they stepped inside. When the doors closed, he smiled. "And I missed you."

"I haven't been gone long enough for you to miss me."

"Maybe not, but it was long enough for my sitting room to fill with gifts."

"Isn't it early for gifts?"

"Wedding's about five weeks away. People who can't attend are beginning to send gifts."

"And you don't like your peace disturbed?"

"I'm not *that* bad."

"No. But you like your world comfortable."

"I do. Riley and Antonio are fabulous. I love living with them."

"But…"

"No buts. I love living with them."

"Well, they are filling your house up with gifts."

He sighed and relented. "Okay, the house is different with them there. I want them there. I really do. But I honestly left because I wanted to see you. Our affair is limited. Once they marry, we really will see each other only a few times a year. I feel like these weeks before the wedding are our chance and we should be allowed to make the best of them."

He said it in such a simple, honest way, that she saw his point. Though she'd worried that she was getting feelings for him, there might not be anything to be concerned about. After the wedding, they'd see each other four or five times a *year* at most.

Even if she fell madly in love with him, they'd drift apart simply by virtue of the fact that they lived on two different continents and their feelings would lessen naturally.

The elevator stopped and they got out. Lorenzo pointed out the glass door. "I have a car on the street."

"Okay. But my condo's not that far."

He batted a hand. "We'll take the car anyway. Then I can send the driver back to his company."

They got into the car and were driven the few blocks to her condo. Using his phone, he paid the bill. The driver retrieved Lorenzo's black duffel bag from the hatch, and they headed into her building.

They entered the lobby with its sleek mid-century modern décor and walked to the elevator. She pushed the button for her floor and the doors slid closed.

She thought of their last night together but actually took herself back the whole way to that afternoon with pizza in bed. They'd talked about important things, and she'd felt a connection that had scared her. But she'd worked all that out in her head and after the confusing morning she'd had, it was great to see somebody who understood her. She might not tell him about the intake visit, but she didn't need to. She simply needed a few hours of being herself, not caring about the past or the future.

And he would provide it.

The elevator doors reopened. She led him out and down the hall to her condo.

They walked inside. He dropped his duffel bag on the floor and gasped. "Wow. Look at that view!"

"I'm sure you've had a similar one in hotel rooms other times you've been to the city."

He laughed. "Yes. But there's something different about a hotel room view. It's always temporary. This view is yours."

She acknowledged that with a tilt of her head. "True."

He slid out of his overcoat and laid it across the back of her white sofa, then removed his suit jacket.

"Want a drink while I find takeout menus so we can get dinner?"

He winced. "Probably not. I stayed up on the plane so I could get on Manhattan time and bourbon might put me to sleep."

She laughed and pulled a handful of menus out of a drawer in the kitchen of her open floor plan living area. He might live in a mansion, but she'd paid a pretty penny for this condo then completely remodeled it. The dark bamboo flooring gave a cozy feel to the space and complemented her white sectional sofa with two yellow throws, as well as the white cabinets in the kitchen.

"Here you go." She handed the menus to him, walked to the smoky-blue-colored tile fireplace and pressed the button that turned on the gas. A small fire sprang to life.

Lorenzo loosened his tie and unbuttoned the top two buttons of his white shirt before he flipped through the takeout menus. "What's your preference?"

She loved how relaxed he looked, especially since he appeared perfectly at ease in her home.

Actually, he fit. For as much as he belonged in his villa, he also fit in her condo.

"I skipped lunch so I'm starving. Wanna get burgers?"

"You sound like Marco."

"What then?"

"It's cold. How about soup?"

"I know just the deli."

She walked to the kitchen island, got her purse and rummaged for her phone. As she dialed the number, he glanced around, smiling with approval. Though his opinion shouldn't matter to her, it gave her great pleasure that he liked what he saw. Particularly since she'd done all the decorating herself.

She ordered soup with some breadsticks. When she was done, she offered him a bottle of water. He took it happily.

"So?" She sat on the sofa. "Who's doing your work while you're away?"

"I can do a lot online, but Antonio had meetings scheduled with our lawyers here in Manhattan." He chuckled. "I made it seem like I was doing him a favor by taking them so he could stay in Florence with Riley."

She gasped. "You devil."

"Hey, I *am* doing him a favor." He eased onto the chair across from her. But she didn't care that he hadn't sat beside her. This gave her a good chance to look at him. The comfortable way he sat forward, elbows on his knees, hands folded in front of him. While she'd ordered their soup, he'd rolled up the sleeves of his white shirt and now looked like the businessman that he was, sleeves out of his way so he could get down to work.

"He also didn't argue about taking a bit of my work while I'm away."

She laughed. "That just makes sense."

"Especially since it ensures he gets private time with Riley."

She laughed. "And that makes even more sense."

When Juliette's landline rang, Lorenzo watched her push herself off the sofa, walk to the kitchen and answer it. She said "Okay" a lot, then reached for her purse again.

"That was the doorman. Our soup is here. He'll bring it up."

A minute later, there was a knock on the door. The doorman entered with two brown paper bags. She tipped him and closed the door.

He rose. "Where do you want to eat?"

"You're tired. Let's sit on the sofa."

"It's white."

"That's what the throws are for."

"They're yellow."

"I'll wash them."

He laughed. "You're so casual about these things."

"Because I know how to use a washing machine."

She set the soup and breadsticks on the center island. As she pulled the breadsticks out of the bag he said, "So, are you going to tell me what's happening with Greg's parents?"

She said, "Nothing. Really," but she slid a breadstick out of the bag and took a big bite.

He sniffed. "Stress eater?"

"No." She winced. "Maybe." Looking like a lost lamb, she eased down to sit on one of the stools in front of the island. "I don't want to burden you. Mostly because it was nothing."

"*What* was nothing?"

"I did the intake interview."

"Oh." He'd suspected she wouldn't be able to send someone else to handle that meeting if she'd arrived in time to go herself. Curiosity overwhelmed him and he sat on the stool beside hers. "What happened?"

She rose and went to a cupboard and opened it, leaving her back to him. "We keep the interviews short. We don't overburden the potential clients. I spoke with both Walter and Rachel—just long enough to assess their conditions and what they'd need." She walked back to the counter with two soup bowls and filled both with soup, then handed one to him.

"And what did you think?"

She walked away to retrieve soup spoons and he realized that she needed to be doing something—not looking at him—to be able to talk about this.

Because it confused her? Because she was embarrassed to talk about it? He didn't know.

"My analysis was that they're old and sick." She sat on her stool beside him. "And alone."

He caught her arm to get her attention. "Hey, that's not your fault. You would have happily let them into Riley's life."

"I would have. Even if they didn't want anything to do with me, I would have let them love Riley."

"And it confuses you that they didn't want that?"

"Yes! I was alone after my parents died. I would have given anything to have family in my life. When Riley was born, I finally had a connection again."

He said, "Yeah. I get it."

They ate a bit of their soup in silence. Then she sighed. "Did you ever wonder why fate showed you something?"

"You mean you think it's fate that yours is the agency their doctor chose?"

"Yes."

He shrugged. "I have two thoughts. First, your agency is very good. That's why their doctor thought of you. And second it only means something if you make it something. What if it really is a coincidence that you are connected to them again…and what if you try to make it something that it isn't? The only thing you will accomplish is lost sleep."

"I never thought of it that way."

"Well, think of it that way. Sometimes a co-incidence really is just a coincidence."

He tossed his napkin on the counter. "That's enough serious talk. Time for a break. What do you say we dance?"

Her eyes widened, then narrowed, as if she wasn't sure she'd heard him correctly. "What?"

"Dance." He retrieved his phone and pulled up a playlist. "Surely you've heard of it."

"Yes. But…dance? In a kitchen?"

"Kitchen, living room, bathroom. What does it matter? When someone needs cheering up, who cares what room you choose?"

She laughed. "I can cheer myself up."

"Ah. Why would you want to do that when dancing is so much fun? For once, give yourself a break. Stop worrying and wondering and just dance." A slow romantic song floated into the room. He offered his hand to her.

She sniffed. "That sounds like a line."

"I never use lines. I always say what I think."
He offered his hand again.

"Well, if it's not a line—" She took his hand.

He pulled her close. He almost said, "There.
Isn't that better than trying to figure out everything?" But holding her felt so good, he decided
to let the moment speak for itself. He genuinely
believed it was a coincidence her ex's family had
hired her firm, but he also understood how that
could open emotional doors for her.

With the size of her open-plan area, he could
maneuver her away from the island into an un-
cluttered space between the kitchen and the living area. The music drifted around them. He felt
the stress of the day and his tiredness melt away.

"This is better."

He smiled down at her. "I do have a good idea
or two every once in a while."

She laughed, easing closer and laying her head
on his shoulder.

He tightened his hold on her to accommodate
her. Her softness pressed up against him and his
eyes closed. He allowed himself to feel every
sensation, absorb every scent, enjoy every word
and note of the song.

Her hand cruised up his back. His hand slid
up hers then down again.

There was a natural intimacy between them,

something he couldn't deny, even if it sometimes baffled him. They'd known each other for a few weeks and he felt like he'd known her forever.

Juliette felt like she was floating. As a woman who kept her boyfriends and lovers at a distance, she didn't have moments like this. Quiet intimacy. Not because she liked Lorenzo more than the rest, but because there was something different between them. More than lust, not as unreliable as love, it was sort of a bond—a link—something unique and wonderful.

The music stopped. She looked up. He gazed down at her with such longing that her heart stuttered. Their lips drifted toward each other naturally and met warmly. But in seconds, the kiss heated. She slid her hands along his silk shirt, luxuriating in the feeling of the fabric and muscles beneath. Sweet arousal rippled through her. Her entire body begged for attention. As if reading her mind, he deepened the kiss. With the increase in tempo came an increase in need. His hands raced down her back and up her sides.

Still kissing, she guided him down the hall to her room. They undressed and fell to the bed like two people so attuned to each other they could anticipate every move.

It wasn't as hot as their first time had been or as emotional as their afternoon at the hotel eating pizza on the bed and talking about their lives. This time, they seemed to find that perfect combination of familiarity and excitement. Naked and happy in her own bed, she let herself play to her heart's delight, until Lorenzo took the lead. His hands cruised her curves, heating her skin and igniting her blood. When he finally rolled her to her back, hiking her hands over her head and pinning them to the pillow, he caught her gaze and smiled at her.

She couldn't help smiling back. Everything between them was always wonderful. How could she not smile?

She suddenly realized she would miss him when the wedding was over. When she only went to Italy for holidays and birthdays or the birth of a baby.

Still, this was how she liked her life. Uncomplicated. Controlled. No chance to be hurt.

CHAPTER ELEVEN

THE NEXT MORNING, she woke in his arms. She yawned and stretched and wiggled enough that she could get out of bed to shower. He finally woke when she returned to the bedroom, dressed and ready to leave.

Taking a long drink of air, he levered himself onto the pillow. "My meeting's not for an hour."

"I have coffee and a coffeemaker. Or there's a little coffee shop about half a block down. You can get a bagel or a doughnut or a breakfast sandwich." She raced over to him and kissed him. "But I have to go. I'll see you tonight." She frowned. "Unless you work late?"

He laughed. "Are you kidding? This is like time off for me. I'll make sure the meetings end before three, so we can have the whole night to ourselves." He turned to slide out of bed. "Is there anything you'd like to do?"

She didn't hesitate to be honest because even if he disagreed, whatever she said would be a starting point to finding something they both wanted to do. They didn't argue or compromise; they figured things out. Which was so comfortable, so honest, even that added to her ease around him.

She never felt she was being pushed into a corner.

"I wouldn't mind a nice dinner."

"I did notice you eat a lot of takeout." He kissed her. "So nice dinner out it is."

"Thanks."

She ran out and he glanced around with a smile. These next few days could actually be fun. Or he could even extend his stay until the following Wednesday when they had to return to Italy for the engagement party. There was always something to do with lawyers. They liked billable hours and he wanted to stay in Manhattan for a while.

That night he planned the kind of dinner that they had to dress up for. He'd even had a tux delivered to her condo and a limo waiting in front of her building. She'd swooned a bit when she'd seen him in the tux, and he had to admit she looked so good in her little black dress that he'd swooned a bit himself.

Saturday night they went to a Broadway play, then had dinner at Jupiter and returned to her condo to make love. Sunday, they walked to

Central Park and fed the pigeons. He wouldn't let her work, though she wanted to. He insisted they both needed a break. The air was crisp. The sky cloudy and moody. But the pigeons were hungry and the people watching—something he'd never taken time to do—was more interesting than he would have ever believed. His brain rested, he went back to the law firm with his list of things he wanted to accomplish and damned if he didn't get some real work done.

She headed out every morning around six thirty, to be at her office when her nurses went on shift at seven. He spent leisurely mornings in her condo drinking coffee and eating pastries that he would buy the day before.

By the time Wednesday came around, he was rested and ready to return to a villa filled with gifts and noise, and she was tired enough from all her work to look forward to having several hours in the air when no one could reach them.

They couldn't catch a flight out to Italy until that night. With the time difference and the flight time, they arrived at the villa early in the afternoon on Thursday. Preoccupied with the engagement party, no one even questioned their arrival at the villa together. GiGi was too joyful over having Juliette back to question anything.

Gerard reached for their bags.

Lorenzo said, "Juliette will be in the same room she stayed in last time."

Gerard said, "Very good," and headed for the elevator.

Antonio said, "So why were you in New York so long...what's going on that you're not telling me?"

Though Juliette pretended great interest in digging for something in her purse, Lorenzo didn't miss a beat. "Antonio, your wedding is about four weeks away. You shouldn't be questioning what I do or who I see. You should understand that I'm trying to come up with a wedding gift."

Antonio grimaced. "Right! Sorry!"

"If you bug me too much, I could end up giving you a butter dish instead of what I have planned."

Riley laughed. GiGi shook her head. Antonio winced and said, "Sorry," again. "I'm not usually the one to ruin a surprise."

Lorenzo shook his head. "That's typically my mother's job."

GiGi gasped and swatted him. "I'm sharp as a tack. I don't leak secrets."

Juliette smiled and said, "If no one minds I'm going up to my room for a shower."

"No! Go ahead," GiGi said. "We want you to feel like this is your home too!"

Juliette said, "Thanks," and walked up the foyer stairs.

Lorenzo waited a few minutes before he, too, excused himself. He found her in the room he'd assigned to her the last time.

When he stepped inside, she walked over and kissed him. "I'm not sure if we're getting better at this with practice or if we're just really good at fooling people."

He laughed and lowered his head to kiss her, but Riley came running into the room. Juliette bounced away from him. The move was so fast, and Riley was so clearly focused on whatever had brought her upstairs, that Lorenzo was fairly certain she either hadn't seen her mom pressed up against him or she hadn't registered what she'd seen.

She walked to Juliette. "You dropped this." She handed Juliette her phone. "We didn't even notice it on the foyer floor until it started ringing. It stopped, of course, because I don't have your password to open it. But if it was Pete or Marietta, I'm sure they left a message."

Juliette quickly checked to see who had called, but Lorenzo noticed Riley's attention shifting. Now that the urgency of giving the phone to her mom was gone, she glanced around, taking in everything she saw.

"Nice suite."

"Prettiest one we have," Lorenzo said casually, giving a reason for why he'd put Juliette on this floor. "So, we're a couple days away from your engagement party..." he said, changing the subject.

"Yes! It's a great way for me to meet a lot of your relatives and business associates all at once before the wedding. Plus, I'm excited to meet Antonio's mom."

He didn't overtly react. He could not refuse Antonio the right to have his mother at all his wedding celebrations. But that didn't mean he had to like it.

Or even pretend he liked it. Particularly since Annabelle could behave perfectly at the engagement party and come to the wedding stone-cold drunk and curse at anyone who tried to talk to her.

He didn't worry for himself. He would simply have her escorted off the grounds if it was up to him. He worried for Antonio. His son was happy. His expectations were high. If his mother did something, it would devastate him.

With Lorenzo and Riley chatting in her room, Juliette walked from the sitting room into the bedroom to return Marietta's call.

"I'm at the airport in Rome."

Juliette blinked. "What?"

"I flew into Rome. Now I think I take a train to Florence but I'm not sure."

Juliette sat on the bed. If she and Lorenzo hadn't been so secretive about him being in Manhattan, Marietta could have flown with them. Instead, it appeared she'd taken another flight out.

"Yes. Take the train to Florence." She bit her lip, thinking things through. "I don't know if the family is putting you up here in the villa or if they have you in a hotel. Before I come get you, I'll ask."

"*You're* coming to get me?"

"Sure. I've been from Florence to the villa lots of times." And it was a good way to get out of the house for a few hours and put some distance between her and Lorenzo so they could adjust to the fact that they weren't in her home, where they could do anything they wanted. "I know my way. And I've been driving since I was a kid. The train ride will take an hour and a half. That gives me time to get a shower, then ask about your arrangements and drive into town. Text me the time the train leaves so I'm not too early or late."

"Okay."

Juliette disconnected the call and returned to the sitting room of her suite where Riley and Lorenzo were still chatting. "Marietta's at the airport. She's about to take the train to Florence."

Riley clapped her hands with glee. "Yay!" She faced Lorenzo. "Should we send somebody to get her?"

"Actually, I told her I'd be driving to town to pick her up."

Both Lorenzo and Riley faced her.

She shrugged. "I know the way. Besides, she and I can talk business, then when we get here, we'll be all yours."

"Okay!" Satisfied, Riley pivoted and raced out of Juliette's suite.

Lorenzo crossed his arms on his chest. "You're going to drive in Florence?"

She laughed. "I've got to do it sometime. I've been back and forth a few trips and I'm actually a very good driver."

"Let me go with you."

"No." As she had with Riley, she kissed his cheek. "We need some distance, a chance to shift our behaviors from how casual we were in my condo. I'll be fine. I have GPS on my phone."

"Better make sure to set it up before you leave."

She teasingly said, "Yes, boss," and grabbed her suitcase to roll it back to the bedroom. "Now leave so I can unpack. I want to shower before I get her."

He started out of her suite but stopped. "Take the big black SUV when you go. That's got GPS already set up."

In the bedroom, she began pulling clothes from her suitcase and tucking them into drawers or hanging them in the closet. Without time to shop for a new dress for the engagement ball, she'd brought a red silk sleeveless gown that she'd worn to at least four Christmas parties. Elegant in its simplicity, it always made her feel beautiful. Saturday night, she'd be the mother of the bride, officially for the first time, and she wanted to look her best.

She smiled dreamily. It might not have happened the way she'd expected, but her daughter was getting married to a wonderful man who had a fabulous family. Everything was going well. Without anyone overwhelming her, she felt part of everything—

Mother of the bride. Happily involved with the groom's gorgeous father. Caring for Greg's parents.

The last one popped into her head of its own volition, causing a horrible feeling of dread to shuffle through her. She couldn't understand why the thought of Greg's parents ruined the moment or even popped into her brain at all. They were clients. Nothing else.

Given that Antonio's family was wonderful, Lorenzo made her happy and the wedding filled her with anticipation, Greg's parents should be the last thing she'd think about. Caring for the sick and elderly was her company's bread and butter. There hadn't been any angry words when she'd gone to their home, and they clearly hadn't recognized her. She'd also managed to stay neutral after a few stray memories when she saw the condition of their home.

She would not let thoughts of Greg's parents, the decades-old insults, the shaming, get to her. Not when this weekend could be one of the happiest of her life.

She refused.

She wasn't simply smarter than to do that. She was stronger.

In fact, she was the strongest person she knew.

A few memories wouldn't take her down.

Over three hours later, Juliette stepped into the foyer with Marietta Fontain following her. Both glowing. Both giggling.

Lorenzo had overheard GiGi telling Juliette that arrangements had been made for the maid of honor and best man to stay at Riley's hotel—the name they gave to the hotel in Florence where she'd stayed while she and Antonio were falling in love. So, Lorenzo wasn't surprised Marietta didn't have luggage. They'd probably stopped at the hotel to drop it off.

The tall, wispy redhead impulsively hugged

him, and he laughed. "It's nice to see you too, Marietta."

She winced. "Sorry. I'm just so excited I can't contain it."

"We're pretty happy too," Lorenzo said. With Juliette standing beside him, he almost slid his arm around her waist to bring her close to him, and he stopped cold. Not because he worried that people would see. But because the gesture had been so natural. The kind of thing a man does with a woman he considers his partner, the woman he loves.

If he'd thought his reaction to almost sliding his arm around her waist was bad, the word *love* nearly choked him.

He wrestled it to the back of his mind. Tonight, he and Juliette would sleep together. They'd have the whole nine yards. A lovely evening with family and friends, followed by a passionate night.

He had plans and would not let a few random thoughts ruin them.

His phone buzzed with a text. He pulled it out of his pocket and sighed. "Rico is here."

Juliette said, "Rico?"

"Antonio's best man. He wants to know where to park his car."

Juliette laughed. "He's never seen your auto showroom?"

Lorenzo rolled his eyes. "At least he didn't need GPS to find the place. Let me go out to greet him and tell him what to do."

He directed Marietta to the living room. "I believe bridesmaids gowns are being discussed in there." Riley had excitedly told him they were taking advantage of everyone being in Italy for the engagement party to choose bridesmaids' gowns and tuxes.

Then he addressed Juliette. "You've been around enough that you can be in charge of wine...or mixed drinks."

She winked at him. "We'll be fine."

As he turned to go outside, the urge to kiss her goodbye came so naturally that he barely caught himself. Walking to Rico's Bentley, he shook his head at the slipups that kept confronting him that day. It had to be the excitement of guests arriving and a party being planned around him that had him off his game. Normally, he wasn't so careless that he nearly made mistakes. But now that he was aware, he would watch what he said and did.

Rico stepped out of the car. Tall and thin, the dark-haired British coffee merchant looked perfectly at home in a T-shirt and jeans with a black leather jacket. He caught Lorenzo in a big hug the way Marietta had.

"Good to see you, old man," he said, slapping

Lorenzo's back, his British accent smooth and clear in the crisp air.

Lorenzo snorted. "I'm far from an old man."

"I know. Rumor has it you've got a new lady in town."

Lorenzo gaped at him. "What?"

"I know. I know. It's a secret. The way all your relationships are."

"Not all my relationships are a secret." Actually, they were. "Just drive up to the garage door and one of the maintenance guys will park your car inside. We can text them to get it for you when you're ready to leave."

Rico tossed his car starter in the air with a sarcastic laugh. "Evading the question about your mystery woman." He shook his head. "Same old Lorenzo."

Rico said "same old Lorenzo" as if there was something wrong with that. There wasn't. His life was good, happy, because he kept his most intimate company private. One friend of his son's, no matter how close to the family, wouldn't make him feel weird.

But he addressed it with Juliette that night, when dinner was over, and the kids had decided to go to the wine tasting room and join the tourists for music and dancing. With no one to notice, he and Juliette had gone to his room.

"Do you ever get hassled over keeping your private life private?"

She considered that as he brushed her hair aside so he could unzip her dress. When it was down and the garment slithered to the floor, she sighed. "Yes and no. The people who count, Riley and Marietta, know they'll get the scoop when it's over, so they don't ask and jeopardize their access to the juicy details. Anybody else just gives me significant looks if I come to the office doing the walk of shame."

"Walk of shame?"

"You know—in the same clothes you had on the day before."

He laughed heartily. "This is why I—"

Love. He almost said *why I love you*! What the hell was wrong with him?

Luckily, Juliette stopped his talking by standing on tiptoes and kissing him. In only yellow panties and bra, she brushed a kiss across his mouth, then began unbuttoning his shirt. With one quick move of her hands under the clothes at his shoulders, she removed both his shirt and jacket.

Reaching for his belt, she frowned. "You always wear too many clothes."

He laughed and shoved aside the weirdness that kept sneaking up on him by changing the subject. "I love you in yellow."

"You seem to love me in most colors."

"I prefer you *out* of most colors," he said, sliding his hand under her bra strap as he kissed her.

She all but purred with contentment, the sound hitting the part of him that responded to her naturally and happily.

They made love then she fell asleep nestled against his side. Given that no one was around, he'd persuaded her to sleep with him. She'd agreed but he suspected she would sneak off if she woke in the middle of the night. Which was fine. He only wanted to fall asleep holding her.

For as much as he longed to nod off, he forced himself to stay awake for a few minutes to enjoy the moment. Something was happening between them. He didn't know if that meant it was time to break it off or to wonder if after all these years real love was finally finding him.

He'd been so sure with Annabelle, though, that he knew he wasn't always the best judge of these kinds of situations. His feelings were one thing. The truth of what was happening was sometimes another.

Which was why it was smarter to stay the course. Stick with his normal romancing routine. No more thoughts of love meant no more questions bouncing around in his head.

Besides, she wanted a temporary relationship too. Any decision otherwise might be met with a swift breakup. He absolutely didn't want to lose her until he had to, so he wouldn't bring up anything serious.

He slid down onto the bed, his head now on the pillow.

Even if he was falling in love, he should ignore the potential problems and enjoy it until the inevitable chips fell because they always did. He might usually be the one to break things off, but Juliette was strong, smart, knew her own mind. He had to be ready for the day she said she wanted to move on.

Actually, he should begin preparing for it now. He should stop being so casual and be more intentional about everything he said and did.

Also, as she'd mentioned that afternoon, a little distance between them was necessary when they were here, at the villa. He might be thrilled having her in his home, but he needed to remember their relationship was about happiness. Not love.

Love had never made him happy.

CHAPTER TWELVE

THE FIRST THING Juliette became aware of as she woke was that she was in a different bed. Which was actually her new normal, given that she now spent so much time at the villa—

Except she wasn't in that room. And she was waking up with Lorenzo. She smiled before she opened her eyes and saw him looking down on her.

"Good morning."

She stretched as far as she could with him wrapped around her. "Good morning."

"I have a coffeemaker up here."

It wasn't what she'd expected him to say, but in some ways it was the most romantic thing anyone had ever said to her.

She purred against him. "Sweet talker."

He laughed and rolled out of bed. She'd expected him to initiate another lovemaking session. When he didn't, she realized being on the same floor, in the same room, with everybody else a whole floor below them—or maybe even in the dining room by now—they had all the time in the world.

He gathered her clothes from the floor and set them on a chair. "If you'd like, you could leave a pair of pajamas or a robe here."

"I probably should go to my room and get a toothbrush."

He opened the door to the exquisite, spa-like bathroom she'd seen in the middle of the night. "No need. There are extra toothbrushes and several kinds of toothpaste in the cabinet."

She walked toward him. "I don't suppose you have my favorite cinnamon coffee."

"I might have taken note of the pods on the coffee carousel in your kitchen and instructed staff to get some."

She laughed. "Are you trying to get me to stay forever?"

"Just being a good host."

She slid by him to get into the bathroom and use one of those extra toothbrushes so she could kiss him after. "A very good host."

She opened the cabinet, looking for a toothbrush, and found two white terrycloth robes instead. One was clearly Lorenzo's size, the other was smaller and fit her like a glove. She'd think he'd had it placed in his room, as he had with her favorite coffee, except Lorenzo was a gorgeous, wealthy man. He might live with his family, but he had a private apartment.

She was not the first woman he'd brought here.

Brushing her teeth, she told herself that didn't matter. He wasn't the first guy she'd had an affair with.

Except he was the first guy in a long time that she'd had these over-the-top, happy feelings for. Their relationship was more than just stolen nights or afternoons. They talked about things—they liked each other.

She shook her head, reminding herself that a big part of her extreme happiness was a result of her joy over her daughter getting married. She was planning with Riley and GiGi and had laughed herself silly with Marietta the day before as she'd driven them along the roads from Florence. She was having fun. *Real fun.* Fun that had nothing to do with work or success. She was enjoying herself.

Enjoying life.

Wow. She couldn't remember the last time she'd done that.

After her final mouth rinse, she noticed her hair was sticking out all over the place. She tried to fix it with her fingers but failed.

"Let it be." Lorenzo walked into the bathroom and kissed her. "I like it a bit messy. It reminds me of everything we did last night. I can take that image to work with me."

The shimmer of happiness over the lovely things he always said to her was tempered by the mention of work. She groaned. "You have work?"

"It is Friday, and I did spend over a week in Manhattan with you. Plus, you'll be doing wedding planning so we wouldn't see much of each other anyway. Your coffee's on the kitchen island. I have to get dressed."

She almost asked him if he was going to shower, then thought the better of it. If he had time for shower sex, he would have suggested it. She gave him a quick kiss goodbye, then went on a mission to find her coffee.

In the morning light, his quarters looked bigger and fancier than what she remembered from the night before. A butter-brown leather sofa and recliner dominated the main living space with the big-screen television. Natural wood cabinets and geometric print tile in the kitchen area were complemented by dark countertops. The place was extremely masculine, yet rich and expensive looking.

She knew exactly how expensive from having recently finished decorating her own condo. She found her coffee and turned on the television, not surprised when she was able to find a morning show in English. She listened to the news, drinking her coffee, and rose when he finally came out of his bedroom, dressed for work.

"I need to get going."

She smiled and nodded. "I should go too. I want to shower and dress before breakfast."

He adjusted his cufflinks. "Since Marco's in town for the engagement party, I'm meeting him for breakfast. Then the goof will probably keep me in meetings all day." He rolled his eyes. "You'd think he was my only supplier. Except he uses the time to pick my brain so he can do bigger and better things with his own company. I swear last summer I all but wrote his corporation's five-year plan."

She laughed.

He kissed her quickly, then headed for the door. "I'll see you tonight."

He left so fast the whole room shimmered with confusion.

She took her cup to the sink, then went into the bedroom to gather the clothes she'd worn the night before. The sense of foreboding that she'd managed to sidestep the past few days tiptoed through her. Alone in his bedroom, after the rushed way he'd left her, a horrible thought struck her.

What if the thrill of their relationship was gone for him?

She took a breath, left his bedroom and snuck into the hall then to her room. She didn't need to sneak. No one saw her. He really did have perfect privacy on the third floor, all by himself.

But maybe that was part of what had taken away the mystique for him? With everyone focused on some facet or another of the wedding, no one would notice or care that they were on this floor together and, in a way, she wasn't forbidden fruit anymore.

She thought about that as she showered, telling herself she was making too much out of nothing—

Except if another man treated her this way, that would be her signal to end it before he did.

Was this her signal to end it?

She never let anyone dump her. She never let herself get so involved that her feelings might be hurt. Her subconscious could be telling her she should be planning her escape. Not just because she didn't want Lorenzo to break up with her at the engagement party or before the wedding, when things really could get complicated. But because she was having *feelings*. Bigger feelings than what she usually had for the men she had relationships with.

Of course, if *she* broke up with *him* before the engagement party, wouldn't she be doing the same thing she was worried Lorenzo might do?

She sighed. Maybe this wasn't the time to make that decision?

Particularly since today was the day to choose bridesmaids' gowns.

Caught up in the excitement of the day, Marietta wanted to go into town to the boutique to try on bridesmaids' dresses, but GiGi had exhausted herself the day before. Not wanting to leave Antonio's grandmother out, Riley called to see if the gowns could be brought to the villa, and an hour later Rosalee Agosti arrived, sample dresses in her van.

Gerard helped her unload the clothing rack and wheel it into the living room before he eased himself away from the noisy group.

As maid of honor, Marietta surveyed the gowns, examining every dress as Rosalee pulled it off the rack.

"I like the pink one," GiGi said from the sofa.

Juliette laughed. "I do too, but it's a winter wedding being held outside in a resting vineyard. I think you need a gown as dramatic as the setting."

Riley considered that. "What are you thinking?"

As if catching on to Juliette's suggestion, GiGi said, "The same dress but in a wine color like burgundy."

"Or a stunning red," Juliette said.

Everybody seemed to like that idea.

Rosalee spoke up. "Let me check to see which of these dresses comes in red."

"Remember we have only about four weeks to get them in," Riley said.

Rosalee nodded. "They will be special ordered."

The boutique owner spent a few seconds tapping on her electronic tablet, then she smiled. "These three all come in red."

Riley took the three samples off the rack and she and Marietta retreated to a private room in the back to try them on.

Juliette sat on the sofa beside GiGi. She caught her hand and squeezed it. "This is fun, right?"

"So much fun," GiGi said with a laugh. "Imagine how much fun the rest of our lives are going to be…" She met her gaze. "With you being here for every holiday and birthday."

She didn't want to burst GiGi's bubble but that was really only a few times a year. Christmas. Easter. And the birthdays of Antonio and Riley's kids—who weren't born yet. She was not going to see as much of the Salvaggio family as GiGi made it seem. Which was why her affair with Lorenzo would end when their lives went back to normal after the wedding.

Her stomach plummeted. It all suddenly felt very real—

Except, it seemed that he was already tiring of her. And she refused to stay in a relationship that was clearly over. That was how women got hurt. That was how Greg had hurt her. She felt the sting every time he'd made an excuse for why they couldn't get married. She should have left him after the third or fourth refusal. Instead she'd stayed and ended up alone and humiliated.

So, rather than be sad that her affair with Lorenzo would end naturally after the wedding, she should be glad that their romance had an end date. She wouldn't be hurt. She'd be too busy working. And they'd both walk away with happy memories.

That was what was important. That she could come back, visit, celebrate without any odd feelings between her and Lorenzo.

She squeezed GiGi's hand again. "I'll be here for every holiday."

GiGi smiled. "I consider myself lucky to have you as part of my family."

"It's fun for me too." Juliette wasn't really lying to GiGi. Her relationship with Lorenzo had nothing to do with her being a part of family celebrations. When it ended, she would still be Riley's mom, Antonio's mother-in-law, grandmother of their children. Right now, she was doing exactly what she was supposed to be doing. She shouldn't be thinking about Lorenzo at all.

She enjoyed her friendship with GiGi.

She loved planning the wedding.

She was thrilled that Riley was happy.

The other feelings? The concerns she had about her relationship with Lorenzo? Those feelings—those worries—had no place here.

After having Marietta try on all three dresses that came in red, Riley chose a long-sleeved gown for her, and Rosalee ordered it on her electronic tablet.

Giggling with happiness, Riley and Marietta decided to take the SUV into town to get lunch. They invited Juliette and GiGi to join them, but GiGi declined.

Juliette glanced at her, saw her tired eyes and said, "I think I'm going to bow out too." She hugged Riley. "You guys have fun."

"Yes," GiGi said. "Your mom and I should go down to the ballroom and discuss decorations for the engagement party."

"Exactly," Juliette said.

With Gerard's help, Rosalee packed up to leave, and the bride-to-be and her maid of honor shuffled off to Florence, their big black SUV following behind Rosalee's van.

When the room was quiet, Juliette said, "Do you really want to look at potential decorations for the ballroom? Won't your staff do that?"

"The decorations, yes," Lorenzo said, entering

the room. "But we have several different kinds of silver and at least ten options for tablecloths."

Juliette started at the sound of his voice. "I thought you were at work?"

"I was. Marco met a woman last night so he's busy, and everything else I had to do today could wait. I came home to help."

Her heart lifted. But she stopped it, suddenly realizing the truth of what she'd thought only minutes before. Her feelings for Lorenzo had no place when they were around other people in the villa, working on wedding things. She had to stop letting her feelings for Lorenzo as a lover mix into her feelings for him as Antonio's dad and GiGi's son… Riley's future father-in-law.

This was the problem. Not that she liked Lorenzo too much. But that she wasn't separating her romantic feelings for Lorenzo from her feelings about the wedding and the new life she was creating as an in-law.

GiGi rose shakily. "Let's go take care of the necessities for the ballroom."

Obviously seeing her exhaustion as Juliette had when the girls asked them to join them in town for lunch, Lorenzo waved her back down. "Juliette and I will handle this. When we get back, we'll all have lunch."

Juliette rose. "Yes. Lorenzo and I can do this."

GiGi sat with a sigh. "Page Gerard. He knows what we have and what looks best with what."

They headed out of the front sitting room and down the hall. When they were a safe distance away, Lorenzo said, "Nothing made me happier than getting that call from Marco saying he was busy today."

She laughed. "Competition for me has officially been ended?"

He snorted. "I won that weeks ago. I'm talking about the fact that I can now spend the day with you."

Her heart wanted to fill with happiness. But she tempered her emotions, testing out her theory that she had to think of him two different ways, as a lover and as Antonio's father. Walking through a main floor corridor to a ballroom, about to choose linens, she should be treating him as Antonio's father.

"Trust me, buddy," she said, bringing their conversation to the place where it belonged. "We have enough work to do this afternoon that you're going to wish you were with Marco."

He laughed and opened the door to the ballroom. They walked through the enormous space and into a room in the back that was filled with dishes and utensils. Gerard was already there, waiting for them.

"Wow."

Every time she came to Florence, something reminded her she was a fish out of water. She felt foolish being squired around in a limo. She'd had to read up on how she was supposed to deal with household staff. She knew what fork to use. She had good manners. But their lifestyle was beyond the commonsense of her world.

Now here she was again, in a situation that was over her head. Mostly because she didn't have any idea what the criteria was for choosing from among all the different patterns of china and silver, tablecloths and chair covers, and vases—hundreds of them. She had good china and everyday dishes. Good silver and everyday silver.

She did not have thirty patterns of china and neither did she have a ballroom. She did not, *could not*, entertain hundreds in her house.

Because there was no reason to.

Gerard suggested two patterns of flatware and china. She absolutely wanted one over the other but deciding to let the guy familiar with all these things choose, she smiled brightly but said nothing, deferring to Lorenzo who laughed.

"I could not possibly care less about the dishes. You choose."

She hesitated. Up to now, she'd managed to sidestep any real disasters. So maybe she should just pick a plate style and flatware and hope for the best?

As if reading her mind, Gerard laughed. "There is no poor choice, ma'am. Everything in this room fits the occasion."

"Okay, then," Juliette said, pointing at her favorite. "I think these are beautiful, the prettiest dishes I've ever seen."

Gerard half bowed. "Excellent."

She picked simple white linen tablecloths and white tufted chairs for around the tables, then she and Lorenzo left the storage room and walked into the ballroom. It was so big their footfalls echoed around them.

Gerard made her choices so easy that being a part of making those decisions could have been one of the most interesting experiences of her life, except for the nagging realization that wouldn't leave her alone. She'd never really thought about what being a billionaire actually meant.

It was more than a big house and fancy cars. It was twenty choices of tablecloths, employees silently cleaning or cooking or setting things up for you before you walked into a room. It was also adherence to etiquette and social conventions—things she didn't have to worry about in her world. All she needed was a firm handshake and the normal manners everyone needed to eat at fancy restaurants and seal deals. The bolder she was the better. And she could be pretty bold, pushy even, about getting her own way. A scrapper. That was what Lorenzo had called her. A junkyard dog—

Her chest tightened with anxiety. Was this what Greg's parents had seen when they'd considered her as a potential match for their son? That she didn't have the refinement needed to plan charity balls or Christmas parties—

Good Lord. *Was* that what they had seen? Her inadequacies? How she would embarrass them until she caught on?

She looked around the ballroom as she and Lorenzo walked the final steps to the door. She was raised blue collar. A nurse, who'd edged her way into a life that suited her. Comfortable to be sure—

But not this.

Realistically, the things she was noticing today could also be only the tip of the iceberg of differences between her life and Lorenzo's. She'd never been on a yacht, never been to Paris, never hobnobbed with royalty, but she would bet GiGi, Lorenzo and Antonio had.

What in the name of all that was holy was she doing here?

CHAPTER THIRTEEN

THE NIGHT OF the engagement ball, Juliette stepped out of her suite into the third-floor hall two seconds before Lorenzo did. He looked so good in his black tux that her breath caught as he walked over to her.

He gave her sleeveless red silk gown a quick once-over then caught her elbows and pulled her to him for a kiss. "You are ravishing."

She returned his kiss. "Thank you." Two days had gone by since her thoughts while choosing the dinnerware for the engagement party and she'd spent that time reducing her foolish fears to rubble. It didn't matter if she'd never been to Paris or ridden on a yacht. Her life and Lorenzo's were separated by an ocean. Their affair could end after the wedding. There was no reason to stress.

Though she absolutely adored Lorenzo, realizing their different places in the world only solidified the temporary nature of their fling. She would enjoy it for however long it lasted, then she would be Riley's mother and Antonio's mother-in-law, and she and Lorenzo would be great friends. He might even let her ride on his yacht someday, but she had no illusions about fitting into his world. She didn't want to.

Satisfied, she linked her arm with his and they walked down the first flight of stairs to the second floor, but they didn't continue down that route to the foyer. Lorenzo pointed out a private stairway and they ended up in a waiting area just outside the ballroom. The noise that ebbed and flowed from the room indicated that guests were arriving.

She turned to Lorenzo. "I thought you'd have a receiving line."

"Meh. Some people do. We're not that fussy."

She smiled and nodded just as Antonio and Riley entered. Wearing an ivory gown, with her dark hair piled on top of her head, Juliette's daughter looked every inch the wife of a billionaire that she was about to become.

Juliette hugged her. "You're gorgeous."

Pulling away, Riley sucked in a breath. "Thank you."

"Nervous?"

"It just seems like time is flying to our wedding."

There was enough of a catch in Riley's voice that Juliette swore she heard fear. The noise of the crowd, the ballroom dripping with finery and all the well-dressed people were enough to make Juliette feel antsy…and she wasn't the bride. All the worries Juliette had about fitting in were probably nothing to what Riley felt as the one marrying into this family.

She wanted to take her daughter aside and remind her there was time to pull out of this. But before she could say anything, Riley turned to Antonio with an expression of love. "We can't wait."

Antonio kissed her. "No. We can't."

Juliette blinked. The catch in Riley's voice hadn't been fear? It had been excitement? Totally the opposite of what Juliette was feeling staying in this huge villa?

Confusion made her glance around. Usually, nothing fazed her. Usually, she loved a challenge. That's what she saw in Riley's eyes—the confidence to take up the challenge of being a wonderful wife to Antonio.

She didn't have to worry about her daughter. She had made too much of the catch in Riley's voice because of her own odd feelings the past few days. It was no coincidence that this home—the Salvaggio wealth and position—reminded her of Greg. Of being unwelcome in his world, and then kicked out of their condo after he died.

But she'd learned that lesson. That was why she was being careful about her feelings for Lorenzo.

She took a breath.

There was nothing to worry about. After all, she didn't have to be the happy bride-to-be, only the happy mother of the bride. The house and ball might be big, but her role was small. She could weave in and out of the crowd thanking people for coming, introducing herself as Riley's mother and simply have fun meeting the people close enough to Antonio and Lorenzo to get an invitation to this posh affair.

Then she would go home and return for the wedding to be the same sunny mother of the bride she would be tonight.

Nothing more.

And, no. This was not faking it. She'd been Riley's mom for decades. She was thrilled her daughter was getting married. That was reason enough to be happy, charming and welcoming to guests.

Dressed in a tuxedo, Gerard entered the room. "If everyone would line up, the master of ceremonies is about to introduce you."

He arranged Marietta and Rico, the maid of honor and best man, as the first in line.

"You and Ms. Morgan next," Gerard said to Lorenzo. "Then Riley and Antonio."

Juliette took her place in front of her daughter, beside Lorenzo with a smile. He caught her hand and squeezed it.

Juliette realized Riley had seen. But the master of ceremony's voice interrupted the noise of the crowd, which instantly settled down. He announced Marietta and Rico, then Lorenzo and Juliette.

She smiled, happy to be Riley's mom, and she and Lorenzo walked into the spotlight that led them to the formal table that was just elevated enough that everyone could see the bridal party.

Still holding her hand, Lorenzo helped her up the three steps, then guided her to their places, one on each side of Riley and Antonio, with the bride and groom's chairs empty between them. When Riley and Antonio were introduced, the crowd erupted in applause.

They entered the ballroom and climbed the three stairs. Then Riley and Antonio took the two chairs between Juliette and Lorenzo.

She breathed a sigh of relief seeing she and Lorenzo were separated. Not that she minded being paired with Lorenzo, but the way they'd been introduced almost announced them as a couple. Plus, he'd held her hand. People had seen that.

She tried not to care. Tried to make excuses. But if they told the world they were dating everything would change. She wouldn't simply be

Riley's mom anymore. A guest. She'd be the woman Lorenzo was dating.

Riley said, "So...anything you want to tell me?"

Overwhelmed thinking about how everyone would look at her differently if she were the woman Lorenzo was dating, Juliette needed a second to bring herself back to reality. Then, she smiled and said, "I suppose I should have said congratulations on a beautiful party."

Riley rolled her eyes. "This isn't about me! It's about you! Holding hands with Lorenzo?"

Her fears shot back like a lightning bolt. "We're friends. Plus, I needed him to help me keep my balance as I walked up the stairs."

Riley considered that. Juliette could see from the expression in her eyes that her daughter was skeptical. Still, she said, "Okay," before she faced Antonio who had taken the mic to say a few words to the crowd.

Juliette winced. She never could fool her daughter. Luckily, Riley was being introduced by her betrothed. She rose and stood beside Antonio as he thanked everyone for coming and instructed the group to enjoy themselves because he intended to.

The crowd laughed. People in dark trousers and white shirts began serving salads.

Riley took her seat talking. "I also heard, Cinderella, that you got a new pair of blue shoes after a piggyback ride in the dead of night."

Juliette almost spit out her lettuce. "My heel broke."

"That's the going gossip. Because you are gossip."

"You think I *wanted* to ride on somebody's back on a freezing cold night?"

Riley shrugged. "Could be. I've seen how you flirt."

"That wasn't flirting!"

"Okay."

Antonio said something to Riley, who looked away from Juliette.

She sighed heavily before catching Lorenzo's gaze and nudging her head toward Riley.

Lorenzo had no idea what she was trying to tell him, but she could explain after dinner. They ate a new dish the chef specially prepared for Antonio and Riley and even named after them.

Juliette smiled at that, the way a mother of the bride was supposed to, but her nose wrinkled the littlest bit, the way it always did when confronted by something in his life she hadn't expected. Like the roomful of china and silver. The very fact that she thought some of those things pretentious made him laugh. Sometimes his life *was* pretentious. Even he saw it.

Which was why he loved her condo in Manhattan. Gorgeous, but also a sort of private oasis.

Dinner ended. Many people made after-dinner toasts, including him. They laughed about the fake engagement that became real love and some of the women in the crowd sighed with envy.

For the first time since this whole deal began, Lorenzo realized he was a little jealous of his son. Antonio's happiness caused Lorenzo to think back to his idealistic self, what he'd thought real love and marriage would be and something warm and soft floated through him. He glanced at Juliette and suddenly realized what he felt for her mirrored what he'd thought love should be.

Antonio and Riley left the platform to mingle before the band began to play. He walked to Juliette's chair and pulled it out for her. "Ready to meet some new people?"

She smiled. "Sure, I'm game."

He laughed. "You don't think very much of all this, do you?"

"Actually, I think it's beautiful."

"But pretentious?"

She chuckled. "Pretentious has nothing to do with it. It's who you are. But I also think it explains your mom's impeccable manners and longing for her charity work, even as it explains why Antonio was lonely."

He walked down the three steps and turned

to take her hand. "You see us as being alone in a crowd, huh?"

She paused before easing down the steps. "Not alone in the crowd. You're with your people."

"*My* people?"

"Wealthy. Sophisticated. People who summer in the south of France and go on ski vacations for Christmas. If anyone's alone in this crowd it's me."

He smiled up at her. "You're not alone when you're with me."

"Easy, Skippy." She started down the stairs. "Talk like that takes us somewhere we don't want to go. And you should really pull back on the hand-holding. Riley's on to us."

In that second, Lorenzo didn't care. Too many thoughts were jockeying for attention in his brain. The fact that he didn't care if everyone saw them as a couple. They *were* a couple. The fact that his feelings for her mirrored what he'd believed love should be. The fact that he didn't have to be anyone or anything except himself with her. The fact that he agreed about the pretentiousness of his life. The fact that he understood why Antonio was so happy and so ready to start this new phase with someone he adored. He could see how Antonio's life would be bigger, happier with Riley. And how his life had been richer and fuller these past few weeks with Juliette.

"Lorenzo?"

He turned when Annabelle said his name. Everything he'd been thinking as he helped Juliette down the stairs evaporated as other emotions hit him like a punch in the gut. Failure. Misery when he realized how wrongly he'd judged Annabelle's character and what a love-struck fool he'd been not to see what was really happening.

"Annabelle..."

His ex glanced at Juliette, then brought her gaze back to his, not really dismissing Juliette, but he noticed she hadn't asked for an introduction.

"Antonio hasn't suggested it, but I thought it would be nice...a show of good faith...if you and I could dance together when they introduce the bridal party."

He frowned. "I think Antonio wants me to dance with Juliette. She's mother of the bride, I'm father of the groom..."

Annabelle's chin lifted. "*I* am Antonio's mother. You and I should dance."

"But Juliette and I came together."

"Only because she's staying here. It's not like you're a couple. She can dance with someone else. Marco's here. It would be nice to get him on the dance floor anyway since he's Antonio's godfather."

* * *

Juliette just stared at beautiful Annabelle. Lorenzo had said she was pretty. *So pretty.* And she was. What he hadn't said was that she looked like royalty. For all Juliette knew, she might be. Tall and slender, shoulders back, an air of something about her—as if she knew she belonged here—

Actually, she *did* belong here. That was what she was saying. She was Antonio's mother. Probably born into wealth and privilege the way Lorenzo had been, she rearranged things with the confidence of a person who had every right to interfere with whatever she wanted because she knew the way things should be.

She behaved the way Juliette did in Manhattan. Running her business. Doing the right thing for her clients. Managing staff. Because in her own world, she was the leader. The strong one. Just as in this world, Annabelle was the leader—

The strong one.

Lorenzo told Annabelle he would take care of things and walked away. His ex stared at Juliette.

"I suppose you're his latest floozie."

Juliette laughed. "I'm Riley's mother. I'm also a business owner in the States. Not really a floozie anymore."

She thought her joke could lighten Annabelle's expression. Instead, it became thunderous. "Joke all you want, pretend all you want, but I know Lorenzo better than anyone ever has. I know when he's sleeping with someone. And he's sleeping with you."

Juliette sighed. "I'm not sure what difference it makes. This party is about my daughter and your son. Let's all just be happy."

Annabelle blew out her breath as if Juliette were tiresome. "Of course, you're happy. Your daughter is marrying up." With that she turned and walked away.

Upstart. Gold digger. Trying to raise your station in life by marrying above it.

Suddenly, the things Greg's dad had shouted at her took meaning. She'd never completely understood it before. Maybe pride had blinded her. She'd wanted to make something of herself, and she had, but that was nothing to these people who only saw pedigrees and the sophistication that came with old money.

As Juliette watched her go, Lorenzo returned. "No matter what she said, ignore it. The woman is a piece of work."

The master of ceremonies began to introduce the bridal party. After Marietta and Rico, the MC introduced Annabelle and Marco. "The mother and godfather of the groom."

Juliette spun to face Lorenzo who grinned. "She pushes but I don't always comply."

A burst of laughter overrode her feelings of not belonging, as the master of ceremonies introduced her and Lorenzo as mother of the bride and father of the groom. Lorenzo swept her into a dance hold and maneuvered them out onto the floor.

A person would never know Annabelle was furious because she smiled happily, dancing with Marco.

"See? Everything worked out."

Juliette glanced at Lorenzo. "Because this is her world, and she knows how to behave."

"In public," Lorenzo clarified. "In private, that's not always the case."

"But isn't that part of it? Knowing when to talk and when to stay quiet. When to sulk and dig in her heels or let go?"

"I suppose." He pulled her close. "Let's not ruin a good dance talking about things that don't matter."

She eased back slightly. "I told you, Riley suspects we're more than friends."

He laughed.

"All right that might be funny, but Annabelle figured it out too. She called me your floozie."

He snorted. "She would know all about floozies." He sighed. "And here we are talking about her again, when I want to dance and focus on you." He took a breath. "You know what? If you and I were to behave like a couple tonight, then everybody's suspicions could be confirmed and then it wouldn't matter who said what."

She gaped at him. "Are you serious? What about all the awkwardness when we break up?"

He waited a beat then cautiously said, "What if we don't break up?"

She frowned.

"Juliette, I can't see myself ever growing tired of you."

Her voice failed her for a second. Then she very skeptically said, "Are you asking me to marry you?"

"No!" He paused. "At least not now...but I have to be honest and say that's where I see us heading. Of course, if you're dead set against marriage, we don't have to get married...but we are a couple. A happy couple. As good to each other as Riley and Antonio. We fit."

It took a minute to find some breath in her frozen lungs so she could talk. "No. We don't. We do not fit."

"How can you say that?"

"How can you not see it? Lorenzo, I've never seen so many dishes before or been with a man who has a house big enough to have a ballroom. Hell, I've never even been on a yacht." The song ended and she pulled away from him, her head spinning. "You're just in the happiness portion of a shiny new affair. And you're trying to make it into something it isn't."

"No. I've been unhappily married. I've had my share of affairs. This is different." He held her gaze. "You know it is. That's why you're fighting it."

Her ire rose. "I'm fighting it because I don't belong here."

He snorted. "Why don't you let me be the judge of that?"

"Because you're not looking at us correctly anymore! Take off your happiness glasses and see the truth!"

"It's you who doesn't see the truth."

He walked away and the band began to play a second song, a song meant for guests to join in the dancing. She smiled her way past the couples pouring onto the dance floor as she struggled to get off, to get away.

Recognizing her role as mother of the bride, she sucked it up and made her way from table to table, saying hello and thanking people for coming, especially Marietta's parents who appeared to be the only people Riley invited.

The horrible sense that her daughter was being absorbed into the Salvaggio family competed with the frightening feelings Lorenzo had inspired while they danced. She couldn't believe he could see them getting married. She couldn't

believe anyone who'd had as bad of a relationship as he had—and she'd had—would even for
one second consider committing again.

After an hour of avoiding Lorenzo by dancing with Rico and Marco and chatting with
more guests, Juliette almost bumped into Riley
when they both reached for a glass of champagne
being distributed by a passing waiter.

Her face flushed with joy, Riley said, "Hey,
Mom!"

"Hey, sweetie. Are you having a good time?"

She laughed. "The best. I love Antonio's
friends."

Juliette glanced around. "I'm guessing a lot of
these people are business associates."

"And GiGi's friends."

"Where are *your* friends?"

"The wedding and engagement party are too
close timewise. Most of my friends can't come
to Europe for both. But *everybody* will be here
for the wedding."

Juliette sipped her champagne. The sense that
she was making too much out of nothing filled
her again. Riley was happy—

She was the one who wasn't. And she suddenly knew why. She liked her life where she
was the ruler of her world. Where she didn't
worry about eight different sets of dishes or flatware or have all these feelings of inadequacy.

Because, she realized as she left the ballroom, Lorenzo's talk of forever hadn't scared her as much as it had made her long for something that couldn't be.

Even if she were head over heels in love with him, it wouldn't matter. She did not belong in his world.

She knew that because she *did* belong in her own.

CHAPTER FOURTEEN

LORENZO GAVE JULIETTE a good hour to get her bearings after their discussion on the dance floor. He knew he'd been suggesting something that she would need time to adjust to, but he also knew he was correct. What was happening between them wasn't a short-term fling. It was permanent. Real.

And the best relationship he'd ever had because she was honest, innocent in a way, worldly in others. She was one of the first people he could be himself with. A mere ten minutes with Annabelle had reminded him of how important that was.

As if thinking her name had summoned her, his ex-wife was suddenly by his side. She made a pouty face. "I think I might have insulted Riley's mother."

"She's tougher than she looks."

Her pouty face got even poutier. "She might be, but she doesn't belong here. She and I both know it."

Lorenzo's heart stuttered. "What did you say to her?"

She straightened regally. Her pouty face was replaced by a look of strength and stubbornness. "I am Antonio's mother. Do not think you and that prissy upstart from America are going to edge me out."

"No one wants to edge you out—"

"Oh, Lorenzo, you're so innocent when it comes to women. Of course, she wants to edge me out."

"She feels sorry for you."

Annabelle gasped.

"Because she's a good person. She doesn't want your place in Antonio's life any more than she wants a place in mine."

The truth of that hit him so hard, he almost buckled over in pain. He wanted her in his life, but she didn't want to be in his.

Why would she?

His family had all but taken over the wedding. His ex-wife, Antonio's mother, was an unmitigated snob. His whole world dripped with money and pretense, and she was a worker bee. She made her own place in the world. She'd made herself who she was.

The very reasons he loved her were the reasons she believed she could never love him.

He waited until the engagement ball was almost over before he looked for her again. He wasn't sure time would fix the gap between their ways of thinking, but he tried to be an optimist. Once he found her, he could take them back to their normal relationship. Then he would wait to mention the possibility of them being together for longer than they'd originally assumed. He would use time to show her they belonged together. Everything would be fine. He simply had to be patient.

His hope dimmed when he didn't find her anywhere in the ballroom. As the guests left, the crowd thinned until he found himself alone in the huge room, listening to the sounds of silence.

It dimmed even further when he walked up to the third floor, sliding his tie from around his neck, and saw the door to her quarters was open. It was a sign to the housecleaning staff that a guest had gone, and they should clean the room.

She'd gone.

He stood staring at the beautiful sitting room, thinking how ridiculous he was to be standing there, looking for her. She wasn't there. The room itself meant nothing without her in it.

His life stretched before him every bit as empty as her room because he was fairly certain that leaving was her way of breaking up with him.

He wasn't sure what he'd tell Riley, but the next morning he discovered that he hadn't needed to worry. Juliette had texted her and told her that her office had called with an emergency, and she had gone back to Manhattan.

Antonio, GiGi and Riley didn't think anything of her packing up and leaving. But he knew what had happened. He'd scared her.

Or his life had scared her.

But the bottom line was, she wanted no part of him.

He'd never been so hurt or so confused. When he'd divorced Annabelle, he'd never been so relieved. He'd begun to see breakups as happy things, but Juliette leaving him gutted him.

Monday evening, Lorenzo said goodbye to Marietta in the foyer before Riley and Antonio left with her to take her to the train station. GiGi sighed, saying she was tired and heading to bed.

In two minutes, he was alone in silence. Just as he'd been in the ballroom after everyone left the engagement party. He almost went to the sitting room to pour himself a bourbon but decided it would be easier to simply make himself a drink in his room where he could find a movie and relax. The weekend had been filled with noise and people, the way Antonio wanted the house to be forever, teeming with kids and laughter, and though it was one kind of wonderful, it certainly wasn't restful.

Still, GiGi and his father had been just fine with him and Annabelle living with them after they married. Of course, Antonio's mom hadn't lived with them long. In a few short years, it had been him and Antonio with his parents, and his mother had taken over the role of mom to Antonio. It had worked out really well because he had needed their help, and they happily gave it.

But Antonio and Riley wouldn't split up after a few years. They would go the distance. They would fill this villa with kids—

He would be a fifth wheel.

Telling himself he was being overly dramatic, he walked up the stairs to his suite, but the sense that he didn't belong here wouldn't leave him. If Juliette had agreed with his proposition at the engagement party, they could live here as the doting grandparents to Antonio and Riley's kids. Somehow that made sense. But him living here alone…damned if it didn't seem wrong.

In his sitting room, he found a movie and sank into the soft sofa with a sigh of relief. He took a sip of bourbon, then another, through the film's opening credits, thinking about Juliette. It didn't insult him that she wanted no part of his life. He understood. She had built her life from the ground up and it was a good life. She wasn't just fulfilled; she was happy.

And she'd done it all on her own. He understood the pride she had in herself.

The movie began. He hunkered down to watch but after a few minutes, he glanced around his place. They hadn't spent a lot of time together in his suite but he could sense her presence.

Or maybe he just missed her?

He did miss her. But not in the way he'd expected. He thought he'd be remembering her in his bedroom. Instead, he thought about dancing with her in her condo. He laughed remembering lying to Antonio, saying he'd gone to Manhattan to arrange for a wedding gift for him. And laughed some more thinking of how they'd had the entire third floor to themselves—

Still, Juliette had told him that Riley had figured it out. That had been the beginning of the end. That had been when he'd suggested that they should just tell everyone and be a couple at the engagement party and she'd refused—

Of course, she'd had a private chat with Annabelle right before that. And his ex could be mean when she didn't get her own way.

Sheesh. No wonder Juliette didn't want to live in his world.

He sat back, combing his fingers through his hair. His house felt empty. Even when Antonio and Riley returned, it would feel empty. His life had been routine and boring for a while. He'd tolerated it because it was a good life.

But now he didn't want it anymore. God only knew what he wanted. He could have just about anything. He was wealthy. That had always given him choices and right now he was considering two changes.

At the end of his movie, he returned to the downstairs sitting room. When the foyer door opened an hour later, he rose and called Antonio and Riley in to join him.

Antonio said, "What's up?"

"Remember how I went to Manhattan to look for a wedding gift for you?"

Riley sat on the sofa. "You're going to tell us you went to see my mom."

He laughed as Antonio sat beside Riley. "Yes and no. I did go to see her, but the visit also helped me figure out what I wanted to give you as a wedding gift."

Antonio raised one eyebrow. "It did?"

"I'm making you CEO."

"Of what?"

"Of everything. I'm going to trade jobs with you."

Antonio laughed. "Really?"

"I'll be taking on all the legal work that requires you to go to the States."

Riley smugly said, "Especially Manhattan?"

He laughed. "Save your suspicions. Your mom made it very clear that she doesn't want to have anything to do with me."

Antonio said, "That surprises me. You two really got along well."

He wasn't about to tell Antonio that it had been his mother who'd said whatever she'd said to make Juliette reconsider the good thing they had. He also wouldn't tell him that in Manhattan he'd have opportunities to run into Juliette and maybe change her mind.

He simply rose from the sofa, said, "Good night," and went upstairs to pack and make travel arrangements.

Juliette settled Pete's problem on Tuesday morning, then crashed in her condo out of sheer exhaustion. At work on Wednesday morning, she opened her laptop to find a message from Greg's parents' doctor that Rachel Finnegan had passed a few days before and that the services required from her company would be changing. The doctor asked to meet her at the penthouse to discuss Walter Finnegan's needs, and she called to let him know she would be right there.

This was what she did. Helped people. She needed the reminder of who she was and why she loved being who she was. Clients and doctors depended on her.

That's what gave her strength and purpose. She wanted to be herself. She did not want to be the pretty woman on Lorenzo's arm. The queen of the romantic villa in Tuscany.

Thoughts of the villa and Lorenzo made her squeeze her eyes shut in lonely misery. But she had understood what he was saying even if he didn't. He might love her, but it was on his terms.

The last time she'd loved a man on his terms, she'd lost him in the worst possible way and been scorned and ridiculed.

She would never do it again. No matter how tempting. Or how much she missed him.

She arrived at Walter Finnegan's building, and the doorman met her, explaining that their doctor had instructed him to input the elevator code so she could go right up.

When the doors opened on the front room, Art was waiting for her. He took her to an office where they spoke briefly about Rachel's peaceful passing then discussed Greg's dad.

"He's been happy having someone to help him shower and dress for the day. Even happier to have company at breakfast and someone to play board games with him for a few hours in the afternoon. Those services should continue."

"If you don't mind, I'd like to talk to him to

get a feel for what he really needs. He's aware enough that he should be the one directing his care. Having us at least consult him should give him a sense of normalcy."

Art rose from behind the big desk. "I understand that. But I also believe he needs more help than he thinks. We might have to guide him to make the right choices."

"Agreed."

They left the office and Art led her to a small sitting room with a wall of books and a television. Walter sat in a recliner watching—of all things—a game show.

"Walter," she said, walking toward him, her hands extended to clasp his when he rose. She couldn't forget this was the man who had shamed and humiliated her at Greg's funeral. Yet, she also couldn't forget this lonely man had just lost his wife.

"Juliette."

A little surprised he remembered her name, she smiled. "I'm sorry for your loss."

He motioned for her to sit.

The doctor's phone rang, and he turned away to answer it. After a few seconds, he left the room.

Walter said, "Must be important."

She nodded. "Must be."

"But maybe it's good we got a minute alone."

His eyes closed and he sighed before he opened them again. "I know who you are."

"I'm sorry?"

He swallowed. "I know who you are. Oh, you don't look the same. But I'm an old businessman who has always trusted his instincts. Your name nagged at me for a couple of days, then I hired a private investigator."

She gaped at him. "A private investigator?"

"I checked you out, and while Art's out of the room it's a good time to tell you that this—" He motioned around the room. "Won't work. If you think a few weeks of kindness will cause me to put you or your bastard child in my will, you are mistaken."

Torn between the urge to tell him to settle down, she didn't want his money, and the urge to stand up, take her nurse and go—right after she told him to go to hell—she sat there staring at him.

"Oh, you were so clever, giving us your best nurses, pretending to like us when you interviewed us." He shook his head. "Do you think I haven't dealt with a hundred women like you who came sniffing around after Greg, or a hundred upstart businessmen who tried to get on my good side?" He snorted. "You're even more witless than we thought."

All the times she'd felt sorry for him popped

into her head, along with the way she'd thought his wife had been the rude one. A million biting comebacks rose to her tongue, but she stopped them. He was alone. He was old and at the end of his life. If he wanted to drown in his own vitriol, that was his choice. Because money did not give anyone the right to be condescending and hateful.

She thought of GiGi. Her warmth. Her kindness. The way she always opened her home.

She thought of Antonio, learning the family business but also creating a family. Building a life.

She thought of Lorenzo. He carried as much weight on his shoulders as Walter did, but he trusted people. She'd never seen him be disrespectful.

Walter didn't need to be either. He *wanted* to be.

She rose. "Walter, you were rude and thoughtless thirty years ago. You are rude and thoughtless now. My nurse will be out of here at the end of her shift. I'll give Art the names of two other nursing agencies who are as competent as mine. I won't leave you in a lurch, but I won't take this from you anymore."

She headed out of the office.

He yelled, "You're still no one. A little money doesn't give you class."

She stopped and looked at him. "You're right about that. Money certainly didn't give you any class. Or any smarts. Riley, your granddaughter, is the nicest, most wonderful woman. Knowing her would have brought you great joy. You live in an empty penthouse with only servants to keep you company. Riley would have loved you."

She turned to walk out, and he sputtered something, but she didn't hear him. She didn't care to hear him. The world and the obvious had suddenly opened up to her. None of her confusing relationship with Greg had ever been about her. It had always been about the Finnegans. Were she to guess she would say they'd somehow kept Greg from marrying her.

Which was every bit as sad for Greg as it was for her. He'd loved her. But he couldn't go against his parents' wishes. She'd always wanted to believe that. Now she did.

Still, that didn't make her a good match for Lorenzo. She had to be who she was, and she could never be herself with him.

In fact, if Greg had married her and she'd become part of his life with his parents, her life would have been hell.

Maybe, by not marrying her, he'd actually done her a favor.

She finished her workday with no residual anger toward Walter and finally accepting that she and Lorenzo weren't right for each other. It hurt. Not because she'd always wanted love but because she'd wanted real love and once again the man she'd found would draw her into a life where she couldn't be herself.

Looking up as she got out of the elevator on her condo's floor, Juliette stopped as if she'd hit a brick wall. There, sitting on the floor by her door, was Lorenzo. He pulled himself up as she approached. Rather than his typical suit and tie, he wore jeans and a black leather jacket over a polo shirt and tennis shoes. In case she'd thought she was attracted to him because he made sexy businessman look yummy, she had now been proven wrong. No man was as handsome as he was to her.

"I think you and I need to talk."

She nodded. Though there was nothing he could say to make her change her mind, she did realize he had a right to hear and understand her side of the story.

She punched her code into the pad beside the door and invited him to follow her inside.

Her heart pounded from the longing that washed through her just looking at him. She reminded herself that wanting him was wrong, though right at that minute she didn't think so. She might not have allowed herself to admit she loved him, but she'd never had feelings this strong for anyone before. Not even Greg. She simply knew better than to enter another relationship where she didn't fit.

He closed the door behind him, as she tossed her briefcase onto the island in the kitchen area.

"I owe you an apology."

She looked at him. "You owe *me* an apology?"

He rubbed his hand across the back of his neck. "I was feeling all kinds of happiness at the engagement party. I spoke too soon about us being together forever." He sucked in a breath. "But now that it's out there I don't want to take it back."

She slid onto one of the stools and offered the one beside it to him. Lord, she wished he would take it back. She wished they could return to their affair, to being happy, to not worrying about tomorrow. Because tomorrow for them wasn't a very happy prospect for her. Leaving Manhattan. Being someone's wife…not being herself anymore.

Still, she wouldn't burden him with that. She'd stick to the obvious reasons committing to each other was wrong. "Lorenzo, we don't know each other very well."

He sat on the stool. "I disagree."

She went to argue, and he stopped her with a kiss. All her feelings bubbled up, not surprising her with their intensity. Her feelings for him were strong and real, but wasted on two people who didn't belong together.

He broke the kiss. Holding her gaze, he said, "What we don't know is the future. I'd like to think we'd be together forever, but I realized I can't make it so by rushing it." He sucked in a breath. "First, because as it stands there are more than a few things you don't like about my life."

She squeezed her eyes shut. "Lorenzo, don't. This is hard enough without trying to fix things that can't be fixed." She sniffed a laugh as she opened her eyes. "Today, I had a meeting with Greg's dad."

He winced. "And you're laughing about it?"

"His mom had died."

Lorenzo's eyes bugged. "Again, not really funny."

"Well, I needed to reevaluate the care Greg's dad would need, given that he is now on his own. When his doctor left the room, Walter told me he knew who I was. He accused me of running a con, trying to ingratiate myself to him to get myself or Riley into his will."

Lorenzo groaned. "Just because Greg's family foolishly threw you away—"

"No. No one threw me away. I finally set things right today. I didn't change the facts or try to fix them, I set Walter Finnegan right. Though I managed to keep myself from telling him to go to hell, I did quit. I gave his doctor the names of two of my competitors and pulled my nurse from his penthouse this afternoon when her shift was over. We are done."

He grinned. "No kidding."

"Hey, I'm nice and I'm fair. But no one accuses me of the things he did without repercussions. He's lucid enough that I knew he understood what he was saying. So, when I quit, I decided to go the whole way. I finished the conversation we'd had at Greg's funeral. I told him it had been his loss that he didn't want to get to know Riley. Then I left." She sucked in a breath. "And it felt good."

"That's because you've spent most of your adult life repressing your feelings about what happened after Greg's death."

"I was busy making a life."

He glanced around her condo. "A good life."

She followed his lead, looking at her beautiful home, knowing she'd worked for every floorboard and lamp. "It is a good life."

"Would you be willing to take in a boarder?"

She shook her head. "Why would I need a boarder?"

He put his hands on her shoulders. "Because I would like time to get to know you. All the time I can get. Us living together should show you that I'm right. We're perfect for each other."

"You are a billionaire who grew up in a villa—"

"Which my son and his soon-to-be wife will be taking over completely. I don't want them to feel like they live in my home. Or that I'm watching them. I want them to have their own life."

His consideration didn't surprise her. She knew he was like a guardian taking care of things behind the scenes. She also knew he saw more than he said. It was one of the reasons she liked him so much.

And now here he was, homeless, on her doorstep.

Her heart thrummed. "Are you saying you're leaving your life for me?"

"Yes. I want the chance to get to know you… the chance to have the happiness that's always eluded me. I found it with you. I want it forever."

She searched his eyes. He was giving up a lot for her—for them. "We'd live together?"

He smiled and her hope blossomed. He might be accustomed to running things like a business, but a relationship wasn't a job. It was life. It was making a life.

"I don't need the big house. I can take over most of the legal things Antonio does with our law firm here in Manhattan—"

"Meaning, you would be working here?"

"And living here…except when we want to visit the kids."

"And grandkids."

He nodded. "And grandkids." He took her hands. "When I realized how much I'd pushed you, how often my family takes it for granted that our way is the right way, I finally saw how much compromising Antonio and Riley had done. Because sometimes you have to compromise to have what you want. I would like to do that with you."

She squeezed his fingers. Her hope was so strong that her voice vibrated. "I would like to do that with you."

"So should we get a pizza?"

She laughed and bumped her forehead against his. "How about a nice dinner out?"

He looked a little disappointed, but said, "Okay."

"That was a test! What I'd really like is about two hours in bed with you, followed by Chinese food that we have delivered."

"I could get on board with that."

She brushed her hand over the front of his soft leather jacket. "It looks like you might be wearing more clothes than I am again."

He shrugged out of the jacket and tossed it into the living room. "I never did like that coat."

"If you're going to live with me, you're not allowed to just throw clothes around."

"What if I hire a maid?"

"What if you don't? What if we live like two Manhattanites, go to a Broadway show or a museum every weekend, eat at fancy restaurants, maybe ice skate in Rockefeller Center?"

"Sounds great."

"It *will* be great." She leaned in and kissed him, and he kissed her back. Their attraction popped. But her heart engaged. This time she let it. If she was ever going to take a risk with someone, it would be him.

It *was* him.

Because when she kissed him, it didn't feel like a risk at all. It felt right. The whisper of destiny that rose up was suddenly welcome.

They were going to go the distance. They were simply going to take their time about it.

EPILOGUE

CHRISTMAS MORNING, Lorenzo and Juliette walked down the stairs, through the foyer toward the sitting room.

He caught her hand. "Ready?"

She brushed her hand along the front of his cashmere sweater. "As ready as I'll ever be."

"The kids knew I was going to Manhattan to see you but since we got in so late last night, this is our first meeting with them knowing for sure we're a couple."

She laughed. "They guessed."

"Yeah, but they haven't really seen us behave like people in love."

"I guess they will this morning."

He caught her hand and they walked into the sitting room, which had been decorated for the holiday. Tinsel had been strung across the fireplace mantle. A huge tree sat in front of the big window facing the circular driveway. Christmas carols drifted out from the speakers around the room.

Riley saw them first. "Mom?" She raced over

and hugged Juliette. "I didn't think you were coming!"

"You thought I'd miss Christmas?"

She stepped out of the hug and Lorenzo took Juliette's hand again.

Riley blinked, but she didn't say anything.

Juliette laughed. "Yes. You guessed right." She smiled at Lorenzo. "We're an item. Lorenzo is officially living with me in Manhattan."

Antonio walked over. "Wow. We didn't have any idea things had gone that far."

Juliette smiled. "We're having fun."

"And it's glorious," Lorenzo said as he headed for the bar.

"So, you're living together in Manhattan?" GiGi asked from the sofa. Then she sighed. "I loved Manhattan. The park. Broadway. Wonderful restaurants."

Lorenzo said, "It's convenient for my new job."

"But we might not just live together forever," Juliette said, smiling at him. He winked.

Catching on long before the Salvaggios did, Riley's gaze flew to Juliette's hand and bounced back to her face when she saw the ring. "You're engaged?"

"Nope. It's a promise ring."

Antonio frowned. "What's a promise ring?"

Juliette took the glass of wine Lorenzo handed her. "It's a promise that we'll have a future."

Riley groaned.

Lorenzo laughed. "We're being unconventional. Both of us tried being normal and got stung. So, we're doing everything differently."

With everybody's curiosity satisfied, he changed the subject to Antonio's first week as the new CEO. Antonio had a lot to say, questions for his dad, the man he'd replaced.

Juliette took a seat by GiGi, who hugged her and filled her in on some new wedding details. Riley started distributing gifts from under the tree.

The ease of it suddenly hit Juliette and she swallowed hard. She hadn't had a real family since her parents died when she was eighteen. Now she had one. A great man, a future son-in-law and a sort of mother-in-law who actually liked her.

In a year or so, there would be a grandchild and who knew how many after that. She and Lorenzo had already discussed going to Paris. He'd told her about having fun with the tourists who frequented their wine tasting rooms. He'd mentioned a yacht.

But all on her timing.

The rest of her life was going to be a blast.

* * * * *